His touch set her unruly pulse galloping again.

What is wrong with me? I regularly get wrapped up in the arms of the most beautiful men in the business. They don't do this to me!

The breeze off the sea was cool. She refused to shiver, but they were walking so close that he picked it up.

"Cold?"

"Maybe a little."

He stopped at once and took off his jacket. Before Jemima could think of a thing to say, he had swung it around her shoulders and taken her hand again, urging them on.

"Better?"

The jacket was surprisingly heavy. The silky lining slithered along her exposed skin like a live creature. She felt embraced by it. Soothed and somehow protected. And so warm! It was like cuddling up in front of a warm fire on a cold night. Like basking in sunshine.

Like being loved.

Oh, boy, am I in trouble here.

THE WEDDING CHALLENGE

Chased to the altar—three independent cousins swept off their feet by the most eligible Englishmen!

Pepper, Izzy and **Jemima Jane** are cousins—with nothing in common except the gorgeous red hair they've inherited from their grandmother! They even grew up on different continents: Pepper is heiress to an American business empire, Izzy and Jemima shared their very English childhood as adopted sisters....

But do they have more in common than they realize?

For the first time in their lives the three cousins find themselves together: as a family, as friends, as business partners. And they're about to discover that they're not so different from each other after all!

Pepper, Izzy and Jay Jay are thoroughly modern women, determined to be ruled by the head, not the heart. Now their lives are turned upside down as each meets a man who challenges her to let love into her life—with dramatic consequences!

Pepper had an unexpected encounter in
The Independent Bride (#3747)
Izzy met her match in *The Accidental Mistress* (#3776)
Now Jemima is the last of the cousins
to find her man—in *The Duke's Proposal.*

SOPHIE WESTON
The Duke's Proposal

The Wedding Challenge

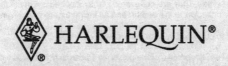

TORONTO • NEW YORK • LONDON
AMSTERDAM • PARIS • SYDNEY • HAMBURG
STOCKHOLM • ATHENS • TOKYO • MILAN • MADRID
PRAGUE • WARSAW • BUDAPEST • AUCKLAND

To Kate

ISBN 0-373-03791-0

THE DUKE'S PROPOSAL

First North American Publication 2004.

Copyright © 2004 by Sophie Weston.

This edition published by arrangement with Harlequin Books S.A.

® and TM are trademarks of the publisher. Trademarks indicated with
® are registered in the United States Patent and Trademark Office, the
Canadian Trade Marks Office and in other countries.

Visit us at www.eHarlequin.com

Printed in U.S.A.

PROLOGUE

THE tall, lithe man leaned on the balustrade and looked out to sea. The simple cottage was hidden away in the hotel grounds, a long way from the hustle and bustle.

He gave a deep sigh of pleasure.

Night. Warmth. A breeze, soft as a woman's breath, across his skin.

Voices wafted over the murmurous water but he was alone. Just as he always was.

So? That was what he had chosen all those years ago. That was what he had stuck with. You make your choices. Then you live by them.

But sometimes, on a perfect night like this, when the air was heavy with the scents of leaves and the sea, he found himself wondering. What if it had been different? How would it feel if she were here with him?

'"The not impossible she",' quoted Niall Blackthorne aloud, mocking himself.

Across the bay, the entrance to Casino Caraibe Royale was lit up like Las Vegas. Already people were arriving in their hired limousines. Pretty soon the steel band would start.

Party time, thought Niall.

He shook himself out of his uncharacteristic reverie and stretched lazily in the gathering dark. He was shirtless, his tanned legs bare under the disreputable denim shorts. At nightfall the air was still warm along the skin. It was only later that the wind off the sea would really get up. And he would go to work.

He grinned, thinking about it. Showered and smooth-shaven, his hair gleaming blue-black in the moonlight, his tuxedo tailored to perfection, he would drive over to the casino. He would circulate among the tourists and the professional gamblers, aloof and mysterious, and play blackjack and roulette and poker.

Sometimes he won, and people envied him. Sometimes he lost, and they marvelled at his cool indifference. But either way they kept their distance. Even the women who fancied themselves in love with the enigmatic gambler never stayed. He never wanted them to.

Now, just for a moment, in the hot, quiet night, he could pretend that he was the beach bum he looked like. There were compensations for being alone, he reminded himself wryly. No woman would tolerate his beach bum side for long. Even if he wanted her to.

And of course he didn't. His grin died. Soberly, he looked at the shifting starlit ocean.

Face the truth, Niall.

He was a one-woman man. And the one woman belonged to someone else.

CHAPTER ONE

THE big, bustling room fell silent when Jemima Dare walked in.

Rooms did that these days. It was no more than a collective intake of breath. But it was more eloquent than a drum roll. It said, Love her or loathe her, the Queen is here.

That was what she was now, thought Jemima. The Queen of this little world.

She could feel the eyes. And the expectations. A wall of expectations pressing down on her. For a moment she felt as if she could hardly breathe.

Then she got a grip. *Never disappoint your public...*

So Jemima Dare flung back the gorgeous Titian hair, narrowed the famous amber eyes and smiled blindly into the silence.

It had started the moment Belinda Cosmetics chose her to front their international campaigns, that silence. Now she was on the cover of this month's *Elegance Magazine* for the second time in a year and her crown was assured. Every model in the room was green with envy—and far too many of them loathed her because of it.

Be careful what you wish for; you might get it.

Instinctively Jemima squared her shoulders.

'Hi,' she said to the room at large.

But already everyone was back at work, adjusting the designer clothes, balancing on cruelly high heels, concentrating on hair and make-up. One or two of the women who'd used to be her friends before she was Queen smiled back. A new girl, fifteen if she was a day, was so awed that she looked as if she were going to cry. But nobody spoke.

Although the room was a furnace, after the ice and hail

in the streets, Jemima felt frozen from her fingertips to her heart's core.

Be careful what you wish for...

Well, she had wished. And she had got it. And not a thing could she do about it, not any more. The die was cast.

It had been cast years ago. She had been seventeen. She had believed Basil Blane when he'd said, 'Babe, you're a natural. I can make you a star.'

And, of course, he had. She was a star, all right. Queen of the catwalk. Imperious priestess of the photo shoot. Basil had just never said what it would cost.

For a moment she looked round this room of women who couldn't even bring themselves to say hello to her and the amber eyes were bleak. Then she shrugged. The price of success, she told herself cynically. She lengthened her panther's prowl and wove an expert way through the racks of shrouded clothes and palpitating assistants.

She had been navigating the backstage chaos of international fashion shows for five years and more. She knew how to do it. There was a job to do here, and she was good at it.

'You're here,' said the designer. His eyes were wild and his hands colder than her own. This was his first big show. 'I called and called. Don't you ever answer your phone?'

Jemima sidestepped the question. 'I don't let people down.' That was true. Almost the only thing in her life she was proud of now. 'Relax, Francis. I'm going to do you proud.'

True to her word, she gave the performance of her life out on the catwalk—a prowling predator in minimalist silks. The show got a standing ovation. The designer gathered the models about him and wept.

Jemima dropped her head on his shoulder. The waterfall of Titian hair cascaded artistically across the front of his leather jacket. It looked spontaneous, friendly, even affectionate. And it would make a hell of a photograph.

Everyone knew that. That was how they had all sat round

and planned it last night. The PR people, the publicist, Francis...

Spontaneous? Huh!

Just for a moment, when they'd told her last night, she had flared up. She was fresh in from Paris, and travelling made her edgy these days. For half a second she'd forgotten that they paid her a lot of money to pretend to be spontaneous.

'You're trying to get a rumour going about Francis and me,' she'd accused them, with more accuracy than tact.

People started to read their briefing notes avidly, or stared round the untidy boardroom. No one met her eyes.

In the end it was left to the head honcho to spell out the facts of life.

'Just do the business, Jemima,' Belinda's UK marketing director said wearily. 'You're the face of Belinda. We need the column inches. Madame's in town for the show.'

And everyone, but everyone, was scared of Madame.

So now Jemima leaned against Francis and smiled up at him as if he was the boy next door, instead of a workaholic dress designer with no known social graces. The paparazzi snapped away, delighted. Columnists scribbled. There was even a romantic sigh or two.

You could see the headlines, Jemima thought dryly. *Jemima in Love at Last?*

She kept her smile so firmly in place her ears hurt.

Once they were behind the curtains Francis removed his arm at once. He looked almost uncomfortable, as if he shouldn't be touching the Queen.

'Thanks, babe.'

He called everyone 'babe', though. That illusion of intimacy was just for the camera. Once the performance was over, they both knew she was unattainable. Every man in the world knew she was unattainable. Except one. And he...

She swallowed.

'You were right,' said Francis, not noticing. 'You did me proud.'

'A pleasure.' Jemima's smile didn't reach her eyes.

'I suppose you don't—?' He was talented and obsessed, but suddenly he sounded uncertain.

She was easing off his last creation with neat, practised movements. One of his staff was helping. But at that she looked over her shoulder.

'Don't what?' She slithered all the way out of the silky tunic and handed it to the assistant.

'Don't feel like a meal later?' he muttered. His ears had gone pink. And not because she was down to her underwear.

Jemima sighed inwardly. Be nice, she told herself. Be nice. It's not his fault he has the social sense of a toadstool.

'No. Sorry, Francis. Madame's in town. I could be summoned at any moment.'

Relief flashed in his eyes. He masked it quickly. 'Another time, then.'

It was so unflattering Jemima nearly laughed aloud. She only didn't because his assistant was hovering. Francis hadn't noticed, but Jemima was more alert these days. She was almost certain that the assistant had a hotline to at least one of the tabloids.

'Mmm, great. Call me?' She flung a sweet, poisonous smile at the assistant. 'Got that?'

The assistant was wooden. She transferred the tunic to its padded hanger without comment. But the air sizzled.

Jemima reached for her bra and clipped herself into it at speed.

Francis blinked. 'You really were great,' he said hastily.

'Thank you.'

He hesitated. Then he said, 'You just get better and better, don't you?'

Jemima was surprised. It showed.

Francis laughed, bouncing into candour on a great spurt of relief. 'Oh, you were always gorgeous. But the last few months there's something new. Like you're dangerous or something.'

She was pulling on silky pantyhose with care, but at that she stopped, startled.

'Dangerous?'

Francis might be socially unflattering but he was a professional. 'It's very sexy,' he said reassuringly.

Suddenly, Jemima was charmed. She gave him her first genuine smile of the day. 'That's really sweet of you, Francis. Thank you.'

'You're better than you know.' He patted her shoulder awkwardly. 'Now I gotta go mingle. Where are you due next?'

This was London Fashion Week, and the models were running from fashion show to fashion show at full tilt.

Jemima sighed. 'Meeting with the PR people. Unless Madame Belinda blows her whistle first.'

'What it is to be a supermodel.' He was only half joking.

'Semi-super. The days of the big celebrity are gone,' said Jemima, pulling on slim tobacco leather trousers and a black cut-away top.

'You could just be bringing them back.'

'Some hope!'

She shrugged rapidly into the matching jacket. It was as soft as glove leather. It would be freezing outside in a London February—but what the hell. There might be photographers out there. The Queen of Top Models couldn't bundle up in winter linings and woolly mittens. However much she might want to.

'And then what? Back to Paris?'

She shook her head. 'I've got a shoot in New York. Fly out tomorrow morning.' At least in theory, she thought, but didn't say.

If Madame Belinda was on the warpath she was quite capable of cancelling a contract at twenty-four hours' notice.

Jemima gave a little shiver. If she lost the high-profile Belinda contract her career was over and she knew it. And then what?

No point in thinking about it. She would have to deal

with it when it happened. So she concentrated on the most important thing she could deal with now.

She snapped huge gypsy hoops into her ears and fluffed out her swirl of shining fox-red hair. Casting one quick, professional look into the mirror, she paused for barely a moment.

'Good,' she told her image. 'Very good. High pneumonia risk, but *good*.'

The designer laughed. He should have been out among his audience, schmoozing the fashion correspondents. But for some reason he still lingered.

'I mean it, Jemima. You're a real star.'

She fished her big shoulder-bag out from among the chaos of bags and shoes on the floor.

'Well, don't hold it against me,' she said flippantly. 'It won't last.'

He goggled. 'What?'

Jemima was already regretting her momentary impulse to honesty. She gave him a wide, photogenic smile. 'Forget it. I've got to scoot. The limo is waiting.'

They air-kissed.

'You really made the show—' he called after her.

But the door was already closing behind her.

The street was crowded with slow-moving traffic, but Jemima spotted her limousine at once. She knew the car. Knew the driver. Insisted that she always had the same one when she was in London. It was one of the reasons she was beginning to get a name for being demanding.

Behind her back they called her the Beast, the Dreaded Diva, the prima donna of pointless demands. They said there was no reason for her list of requirements on transport and lodging and entertainment, that she just did it because she liked to keep people jumping. Because she *could*.

If they only knew.

She slid into the back seat, stretched out her long legs and fished the mobile phone out of her designer bag. She bit her lip. Braced herself. Switched it on.

She ran through the voice messages quickly. She was summoned to Madame Belinda at the Dorchester at three. Well, it could be worse. She did not look at the text messages.

The PR agency were taking her to lunch at the Savoy. Two women, hardly less elegant than she was herself, were waiting on low, luxurious sofas, with a dish of canapés already on the polished wooden table between them. They offered wine, a cocktail, champagne. Jemima declined the lot.

'Bad for the skin.' She sank into a deep armchair with model-girl grace. 'I'll have a glass of water.'

The other two exchanged resigned glances. *Difficult*, they said without words.

Jemima winced inwardly. She had worked with these women for over a year. Her sister Izzy was even going to marry the brother of Abby, the junior on the team. And they still treated her as something between royalty and a delinquent five-year-old. They satisfied her every whim because she was Jemima Dare, the face of Belinda, and every magazine in the world wanted her to work for them. But they didn't have to pretend that they liked it.

Be careful what you wish for...

They exchanged glances again, with purpose. A prepared attack, interpreted Jemima. She braced herself.

'Do you want to check your messages before we start?' asked Abby, confirming her suspicions.

Jemima tensed inwardly. 'No, thank you.'

'Then would you mind turning off your phone? We don't want to be interrupted.'

'It's off,' she said curtly.

They exchanged another one of those looks. Definitely a prepared attack.

Silently Abby handed her a folder.

'Do you want the good news or the bad news first?' asked Molly di Perretti. Not being family, even remotely, she didn't have to mince her words.

Jemima put the folder on the table and sipped sparking water from a crystal glass. 'Good. I'm an optimist.'

Molly tapped the folder. 'Column inches up again. You were the model most talked about in the international press last month.'

'Great.'

'The bad news,' pursued Molly hardily, 'is what they're saying.'

Jemima raised her eyebrows.

'You work less, demand more. You're an arrogant cow and everyone hates you.' Molly's tone was forensic.

Jemima did not blink. 'I see.'

Lady Abigail, who was going to have to walk side by side down the aisle with Jemima behind Izzy Dare one day in autumn, and was not looking forward to it, tried a softer approach.

'It's so easy to get a bad name in this business. You're just going to have to be a bit more careful.'

Molly said nothing. Loudly.

Jemima looked at her sardonically. 'Go on, Molly. Spit it out. I can take it.'

Molly clearly agreed. 'Abby's too easy on you. You're getting a name for being a spoilt brat because you're behaving like a spoilt brat.'

Abby groaned.

The other two ignored her.

'Your demands are getting out of control. It's not just the other models who think you've lost the plot.' Molly started to tick a list off on her fingers. 'You've got to have a limousine you've travelled in before. Drivers you happen to fancy. Private planes instead of scheduled flights. Then refusing to stay in the best hotel in New York because you wanted to be alone, and that meant a private apartment at vast cost…' She glared. 'I've got news for you, Jemima. You're not Greta Garbo. Wake up and smell the coffee.'

Jemima looked stunned.

Abby and Molly looked at each other, relieved. At least they had got through this time.

'Drivers I happen to *fancy*?' said Jemima, outraged.

Or not. Abby dropped her head in her hands.

Molly's eyes narrowed to slits. 'Fine. Don't take our advice. See where you end up.'

Jemima said coolly, 'I pay your company a whole lot of money to run my PR and analyse the results. I didn't take you on as a life coach.'

Molly put down her margarita so hard that some of it slopped onto the highly polished table. Abby mopped at it with one of the paper cocktail napkins. Neither Jemima nor Molly took any notice.

'Okay, I'll tell you the truth—since nobody else will,' said Molly with heat. 'Your agent is too scared you'll dump her, like you did the one before her. And your sister treats you with kid gloves. God knows why.'

Jemima's famously melting golden-brown eyes flickered.

'When Belinda went looking for their new face, they told everyone they wanted someone the professional girl about town could relate to. No more elegant skeletons. No more untouchable celebrities. They wanted a girl who had a family and friends and did normal things. I put some cuttings in your folder,' she added with bite.

'Thank you.' No one could describe Jemima's eyes as melting at the moment. They glittered.

'I thought it would help to remind you. When you got the job, you fulfilled the job description. Now you don't. I'm just betting the people at Belinda are beginning to notice.'

Did she *know* that Madame was sitting in the Dorchester like a black widow, waiting to crunch her bones?

Jemima's jaw was rigid. But she said nothing.

'Oh, please yourself,' said Molly in disgust.

Her eyes met Abby's. The message was clear, even to Jemima: *I give up!* She stood up. 'Abby, you'd better finish up here. I've got real work to do back in the office.'

She stamped off.

Left behind, Abby said apologetically, 'Molly gets very passionate about her work.'

Jemima swallowed. 'Doesn't she just?' But her light tone sounded strained.

Just for a moment Abby thought the beautiful mask might crack. Just for a moment it seemed as if Jemima would come off her pedestal. Abby didn't care what she did—laugh, cry, swear at Molly, throw things…. Just as long as she stopped looking poised and bored and totally, totally indifferent.

But she didn't.

Instead she leaned back in her deep chair, pinned on the famous smile and drawled, 'So, tell me about my family. The last time I spoke to Izzy she said they couldn't finalise the date until Dominic had sorted out his training schedule.'

Abby gave up too.

Over lunch Jemima was barbed and witty, and as defensive as a killer crab. She was charming to the waiters, indifferent to the covert stares of several of their fellow diners. But when one of them got up and came over to their table she tensed visibly, Abby saw.

He turned out to be a lively barrister, with a copy of *Elegance Magazine* in his briefcase and a niece who wanted to be a model. Jemima gave him the slow up-and-under smile that had made her famous, signed the cover of the magazine as he asked, and told him to tell his niece to finish her exams before she tried out for any of the respectable model agencies. Delighted, he gave her his business card and went back to his table.

'Someone who doesn't think you're a spoiled brat?' asked Abby shrewdly.

Jemima was cool. 'Yup.' She tore his card into tiny pieces and dropped them onto the pristine tablecloth. Abby saw that her fingers were shaking.

Suddenly Abby was concerned. 'Are you okay?'

'Of course.' But the golden eyes looked blind, almost as if she were afraid.

Abby leaned forward. 'Are you sure? You looked like a ghost when he came over.'

The beautiful shoulders gave that arrogant shrug. 'I—thought he might be someone I knew.'

'But he wasn't?'

The blind look went out of Jemima's eyes. For a moment she looked rueful, almost the friendly girl Belinda Cosmetics had thought they were getting for their campaign.

'No, he was a complete stranger.' She added almost under her breath, 'Thank God.'

More and more worried, Abby said, 'Jemima, what's wrong? Have you been overdoing it again?'

She knew that Jemima had worked herself into exhaustion six months ago. In fact, if it hadn't been for Jemima diving out of sight for a couple of weeks and Izzy stepping into her shoes Izzy and Dom would never have met.

Jemima looked away, her face expressionless.

'I wish Izzy was around,' said Abby worriedly. Izzy was with Dom in Norway, and wouldn't be back for two weeks. But at least she had got a reaction at last. Jemima bristled.

'I don't need my big sister to take care of me. I can look after myself. As Molly has just been pointing out, I only have to pick up the phone and somebody jumps. It's great.'

Abby sank back in her seat, disapproving and trying to hide it.

She moved the subject firmly away from the professional. Fortunately they had family to get them through the next course.

They agreed that it was a bore that Izzy and Dom wouldn't confirm the date for their wedding. Yes, it was great to see how happy they were.

And then Abby snapped her fingers, relaxing again. 'That reminds me. I've got the Christmas photographs to show you.'

She fished in her bag and brought out an untidy handful. She sorted through them rapidly, extracted a couple, then handed the rest across with a reminiscent smile.

'I'll get you copies of anything you want.'

Jemima did not figure in any of the cheerful pictures. She had managed Christmas Day with the family, but she had been off on a big shoot in the Seychelles on Boxing Day. She flipped through them with the speed of one who spent much of her professional life looking at sheets of photographs.

'All matching pairs,' she said.

'What?'

Jemima fanned out four and turned them to face Abby. There was Abby herself, dancing with her tall, elegant husband, Izzy and Dom, tumbling on the floor under the Christmas tree and laughing madly, and Jemima's cousin Pepper leaning dreamily against her Steven's shoulder.

'Even my parents are holding hands.' Jemima pointed at the fourth.

They were too.

'I see what you mean,' admitted Abby.

'Just as well I'd moved on. I would have unbalanced the party.'

'Oh, come on. You'd have been the star.'

Jemima said in an odd voice, 'Same thing. Stars don't come in matching pairs.'

Abby looked up, instantly alert. 'Still no man in your life, then?'

There was the tiniest pause.

Then, 'Not one I'd take home to Mother.'

The irony was very nicely done. It said, You and I are women of the world; we know that I'm beautiful and sophisticated and my relationships are very, very modern. Much too modern for my hand-holding parents to get their heads around.

But Abby was not quite convinced. 'Are you telling me you're one for the wild men?' she said doubtfully.

Jemima narrowed her eyes at her. 'That's not what I meant.'

'Then what?'

Jemima hesitated. At last she said, 'Put it this way—I'm not looking for a man to follow me round the world.'

'Ah. Yes, I see. It's not easy keeping a relationship on the rails when your work makes you travel,' allowed Abby. Her husband had business ventures in four continents. Even so, he did not travel as much as a top international model. She looked at Jemima curiously. 'Is it lonely?'

Jemima snorted. 'Who has time to get lonely?' It seemed to burst out of her. 'So far this year I've done Madrid, Milan, Barcelona, Paris, London. Now I'm off to New York and Milan again. Then back to New York.'

It sounded grim to Abby. 'You could still be lonely,' she pointed out. 'Do you ever want to do something else with your life?'

But Jemima was flicking through the pictures again and did not seem to hear.

'Hello—what's this one? Been away?'

Diverted, Abby held out her hand for the photograph. Unlike the others, it was a commercial postcard: a standard view of tropical palms with wild surf beyond. She turned it over and smiled as she read the message on the back.

'Oh, that. It's just a postcard from a friend.' She gave it back. 'He stays out of England, but every so often he sends me a postcard to show me what I'm missing.' Her smile was warmly reminiscent. 'Those palm trees look good on a wet Friday in London, don't they?'

Jemima looked at those foaming waves and shook her head. 'Bit energetic for me,' she said dryly, and turned the card over to look at the legend. '"Pentecost Island",' she read. 'Where's that? South Seas?'

Abby shook her head. 'Who knows? Could be. He gets around.'

'He?' teased Jemima. In the square left for messages on the back of the postcard someone had written *Time you tried the white horses!* and signed it with an arrogant black *N*. 'Should Emilio be worried?'

Abby grinned suddenly. 'Not for a moment. He's known

me since I had spots and braces on my teeth. If there's one man in the world for whom I have no mystery it's him.'

Jemima pulled a face. 'Sounds dull.'

Abby laughed aloud. 'He's a professional gambler and gorgeous with it. Whatever else he is, dull he isn't.'

Jemima shuffled all the photographs together neatly and gave them back to her.

'So you won't be taking off to Pentecost Island for a dashing weekend with an old flame?'

Abby was serene. 'Not a chance. I've never even heard of it before.'

'Nor me. Must be pretty remote.'

'Not that remote,' said Abby dryly. 'If he's there, it must have a casino.' She put the photographs in her bag and signalled for the bill. 'Where are you going now? Can I give you a lift?'

'The Dorchester.'

'Nice,' said Abby, her eyes dancing.

Jemima grinned suddenly. 'Not so nice. I'm in for a grilling from Madame.'

Abby's expression changed instantly. She shuddered.

'Now, that woman scares me. I'm so glad we work for you, not Belinda.'

Jemima shrugged again. 'She doesn't scare me.'

'You're really brave, aren't you?'

'Hell, why? She's my employer, not the Emperor Nero.'

'But she can be so *nasty*. And she always looks so—immaculate.'

'So do I,' said Jemima coolly. 'And I can walk away. She can't. It's her company.'

Abby was admiring. But still she shook her head. 'Doesn't she press your buttons at all?'

'Not a one,' said Jemima, her eyes glittering. 'There are things worth getting worked up about. Madame Belinda isn't one of them.'

*   *   *

If she had been at the Dorchester an hour later Abby would have seen that that was not the whole truth. Jemima was getting worked up, all right. But not with fear. With rage.

Jemima shook back her famous red hair as she felt the fury rise. It felt glorious. It had taken a long time. Too long. But now she was *angry*.

She stood up and glared at Madame, the President of Belinda Cosmetics.

'Are you telling me you flew the Atlantic and made me find a space in the busiest week in the year to complain that I haven't got a *boyfriend*?'

The Vice-President, seated at Madame's right hand at the impressive boardroom table, blenched.

Madame President was unmoved. 'Sit down, Jemima.'

But Jemima was on a roll. 'Who the *hell* do you think you are?'

Madame President's eyes held hers. They had about as much expression as a lizard's. They clearly scared the hell out of the Vice-President.

'The woman who pays your considerable bills.'

The Vice-President was theoretically tall, dark and handsome—and very sophisticated. Suave Silvio, they called him on the circuit. Jemima had been on a couple of ultra-cool dates with him, and she knew that his advance publicity was fully deserved.

But now he gulped audibly. Man or mouse? No contest, thought Jemima. She ignored him.

'You don't own me,' she told Madame. 'I have other contracts.'

Jemima looked straight into Madame's lizard eyes, like a duellist facing the enemy.

There was a long pause. Neither blinked.

'And how long will you keep them if I tell the world I sacked you?' asked Madame icily.

Jemima did not let herself remember that she'd already thought of that. She was too intent on the battle.

'And that means you can order me to take a boyfriend?' She was scornful. 'I don't think so.'

Madame President stood up. It was scary. She was five foot nothing of concentrated power and purpose. She slapped her hands down on the table in front of her and leaned forward. Her voice went up to a roar, astonishing for her size. 'You will do what I say!'

It was intimidating. It was meant to be.

But Jemima was in full duellist mode by now. She stood her ground. 'I joined an advertising campaign. Not a harem.'

Suave Silvio moaned.

It reminded her. 'Did Silvio date me on orders?'

Madame made a dismissive gesture.

'He *did*,' said Jemima on a note of discovery. She was so furious she had gone utterly calm. 'And I suppose it was you who put poor old Francis Hale-Smith up to asking me out, wasn't it? I told him to get lost, by the way.'

Madame went puce. 'You are the face of Belinda. If I say you have a boyfriend, you will have a boyfriend!'

'Nope.'

'I pay you!' yelled Madame.

It was the last straw. 'Then I quit,' said Jemima, very, very quietly.

Their eyes locked for electric seconds.

This time Madame President blinked.

Then she straightened and sat down again. The red subsided from her exquisitely made-up cheeks.

'Coffee, I think,' she said, quite as if nothing had happened. 'Silvio, tell them to bring coffee at once.'

The Vice-President leaped to his feet, looking relieved. 'Yes, Madame.' He rushed to a phone in the corner and spoke into it urgently.

What was the old bat up to now? thought Jemima, deeply suspicious. 'Not for me,' she said coldly. 'I just quit.'

Madame waved a hand so heavily encrusted with rings it could have set several small fires if the sun had been shining. Only this was London in February, and the sky was solid grey cloud. Even with lavish windows, the penthouse was safe.

'Good. Good.' She beamed at Jemima, nodding as approvingly as if a promising pupil had just made a breakthrough. 'Sit. Take a coffee with me. We will talk about this.'

She's going mad, thought Jemima. *Either that or I am.*

As much to steady herself as anything, she said levelly, 'When I signed up to be the face of Belinda I agreed to do four photo shoots a year and various PR jobs. I've kept my side of the bargain.'

Madame President snorted loudly.

With a supreme effort of will, Jemima bit back the pithy response that sprang to mind.

When *Elegance Magazine* had first discovered Jemima Dare, one besotted staff columnist had described her as having 'gut-wrenching sensuality allied to Titania's ethereal provocation'. He would not have recognised her at the moment, golden-brown eyes narrowed and spitting mad. But then that had been four years ago. In the interim she had done a lot of growing up—not all of it pleasant.

Madame President was a new experience. But Jemima was a fast learner. And one of the things she had learned was that in confrontations you had to take control.

Right. Give the old bat something to worry about. 'Give me one good reason why I shouldn't walk out of here right now,' she said.

Silvio nearly dropped the phone. Even Madame President looked taken aback for a moment. Then she gave another of those disconcertingly approving nods.

'Because you and I can do business together,' she said simply.

Jemima's eyes skimmed the worried Silvio. 'Not if you were thinking of picking my boyfriends,' she said dryly. 'We don't seem to have the same taste in men.'

Madame's eyes gleamed. 'Silvio, get out,' she said without looking at him.

He went.

Madame was talking before the door closed behind him. 'Okay. Cards on the table. We have a problem.'

Jemima raised perfect eyebrows.

'Oh, sit down,' said Madame irritably. 'It is like talking to a lamp post. Why are models so damned tall these days? When I was a girl in Paris, they were human-sized.'

In spite of herself, Jemima gave a choke of laughter. And sat.

'That's better.'

Madame leaned forward and propped her chin on her steepled fingers. The rings glittered but Jemima hardly noticed. The eyes were not a lizard's any more. They were dark and expressive—and shrewd.

'The press…'

'Have decided I'm a spoiled brat,' supplied Jemima. 'I've just had lunch with my PR advisers. They've given me the rundown.'

Madame shook her head. 'They're wrong. The press enjoys spoiled brats. Our problem is that they are forgetting you.'

She picked up a handful of magazines and flung them across the coffee table. Jemima saw European titles mixed with North American celebrity titles.

'Take a look,' said Madame in a hard, level voice. 'Show me your name. They've got film stars, baseball stars. Even some damned aristocrat who's been missing for fifteen years. How far off today's news is that? But no Jemima Dare. And, more important, no face of Belinda.'

Jemima frowned. But she was fair. She went through the magazines rapidly. Madame was right.

Tom and Sandy: will they split? Eugenio takes us into his lovely Florida home. Where is the Duke? The hunt is on…

She pushed the magazines away. 'Okay. No Belinda. No me. I'll give you that. So?'

'Time to do something about it.'

Jemima's eyes narrowed. 'This is the One Last Chance chat, isn't it?' she said suddenly.

Madame President's eyes flickered. 'Yes,' she said baldly. 'Have you had lots of them?'

Jemima laughed. 'My cousin Pepper is an entrepreneur. We share an apartment. I listen to her work problems,' she said coolly. 'I know the signs.'

Madame looked annoyed. 'Then deal with it.'

Jemima smiled. 'I'd say there was an *unless* coming. You'll cancel my contract unless I—what? Dye my hair? Write a celebrity novel? Sing? What?'

Madame laughed unexpectedly. It sounded rusty. 'I like you, Jemima. You're gutsy.'

I need to be, with sharks like you signing my pay cheque.

She did not say it, of course. She gave her a demure smile. 'Thank you. So spit it out. What do you want me to do? Short of dating Francis, that is.'

Madame was temporarily side-tracked. 'Why not Francis? He's very talented. He'll go far.'

Jemima leaned back and crossed her legs. 'And he's a complete prune. He asked me out over the head of another girl while I was dressed in nothing but a pair of knickers and a lot of sticky tape.'

Madame was startled enough to allow herself to be side-tracked again. 'Sticky tape?'

'He's into deep, deep plunge this collection.'

They exchanged a look of total understanding. In her time Madame President had been a model too. She nodded.

'Ah.'

'What's more,' said Jemima, watching Madame from under her lashes, 'when I said I'd take a rain-check he looked as if he'd been let out of prison.'

There was a small silence. Madame's lips tightened.

'How on earth did you sign him up?' Jemima was genuinely curious.

Madame looked like a lizard about to spit. But she was a good tactician. After a brief struggle with herself, she said curtly, 'Offered him a joint promotion next Christmas.'

'Well, he tried,' said Jemima fairly. 'So, want to tell me why?'

Madame examined her rings absorbedly. 'When we were looking for the new face of Belinda, we had a very specific brief in mind,' she said at last slowly. 'A woman of today— a woman who made her own decisions, a woman with a career, sure, but a woman to whom other things were important too—friends, things of the mind, love, children.'

Jemima regarded her with an unblinking gaze. Then, 'If you want me to have a baby, forget it.' Her voice was hard. 'That's not a decision I'd take because a cosmetic company told me to. Or any other employer, for that matter.'

To her surprise, Madame looked delighted. Triumphant even. 'Exactly. That's the tone I want.'

Jemima flung up her hands. 'I give up.'

'Look,' said Madame, suddenly a lot less dramatic, 'you were my personal choice for the face of Belinda. I liked the way you presented yourself. You didn't crave the celebrity circuit. You didn't worry that laughing too much would crack your make-up. You thought about things and you weren't afraid to have an opinion. I liked that.'

Jemima was taken aback. 'Thank you.'

'Silvio said you weren't glamorous enough.'

Weasel, thought Jemima. *That isn't what he said to me when he was wining and dining me.* Aloud, she said, 'Really?'

'But I said that it didn't matter. This is the twenty-first century, I said. It is time for a change. She lives with her sister and her cousin like a regular person. Besides, they are all three go-getters.'

Jemima grinned. 'Oh, yes, we're that all right.' She thought of Pepper the businesswoman and Izzy the adventure freak. 'By the bucketful.'

Madame grinned back. She was very charming when she grinned, thought Jemima. For a shark.

'So I thought—there's my twenty-first-century woman.

Gorgeous redhead who doesn't spend her life worrying about the size of her bum. Girl with a life. And a future.'

Jemima was touched. 'Thank you,' she said again.

'So how did all go so wrong? What happened to that lovely girl with her feet on the ground?'

Jemima winced.

There was a brief knock and the Vice-President appeared at the door, ushering in a waiter with a huge tray. The waiter poured coffee and glasses of mineral water and left. The Vice-President hovered. Madame waved him to sit. He sank into an armchair with a distinct sigh of relief.

Frowning, she said, 'When that stupid manager started turning you into a professional partygoer, I told Silvio, "Call him up. Tell him to back off." Didn't I, Silvio?'

He nodded enthusiastically. 'You did, Madame.'

'But then you fired him. And I thought, Great. The girl has good instincts. We're back on track.'

Jemima had gone rigid. 'I didn't fire Basil.'

Madame ignored that. 'Only now you don't go out at all.'

'I didn't fire Basil.'

Jemima was starting to shiver, she realised. To hide it, she looked around for her shoulder-bag and fussed through it.

Madame seemed disappointed. 'That's not what I heard.'

The shivers down her spine were turning into a positive cascade. 'I left his management by mutual agreement.'

Madame looked sceptical.

'It *was*.'

Well, eventually. When she had threatened to expose the things he'd done—the pills to keep her thin, the break from her family to keep her 'focused', as he'd called it. Oh, yes, he'd been glad enough to give back her contract when she'd faced him with all of that. Only now he was having second thoughts, and…

If she wasn't careful, she was going to start shaking again.

With another of her abrupt changes of mood Madame lost interest. 'It doesn't matter. What matters is that you have no life. You don't date. You don't go out anywhere unless it's an assignment.'

Jemima was still shaky. 'I work. I don't have time to go out.'

'Make time.'

'What?'

Madame said with finality, 'Go back to being a regular person. You don't have to disappear and come back a duke. You don't even have to date a designer if you don't want to. But date *someone*.'

'I—'

'I'm cancelling the shoot in New York. Take a break. Go meet some guys, like other girls. I want to see you living a life like our customers lead. And I want to see the press stories to prove it.'

She stood up. The interview was clearly over.

Jemima stopped shivering. She was not afraid of Madame.

She tipped her head back. On this dull grey afternoon the penthouse was lit by warm table-lamps. In their light the wonderful red hair rippled like fire, like wine. And Jemima knew it. She knew, too, that the woman who had personally chosen her as the face of Belinda would not want to admit she had been wrong.

She said, quite gently, 'Or?'

Madame recognised a challenge when she saw it. She might like Jemima personally. But she couldn't afford to let a challenge go unanswered. Her jaw hardened.

'We're already into planning the Christmas campaign. I won't pull you off that. But it's your last unless you—'

'Get a boyfriend,' supplied Jemima. Her temper went back onto a slow burn. She smiled pleasantly at the shark. 'I'm almost certain that's illegal.'

Madame did not care about piffling legalities. She snorted. 'Unless you get a *life*.'

'And if I don't?'

The eyes were blank and lizard-like again. 'You're off the team.'

Jemima flipped off the sofa. 'Cast your mind back,' she said sweetly. 'Like I said, I quit.'

She steamed out before they could answer.

The commissionaire summoned a taxi for her. She sank into the big seat and called the agency.

'Belinda and I just fired each other,' she said curtly.

She rang off to squawks of horror.

And then she did what she had been putting off all day. She checked her text messages.

Her fingers shook a little as she pressed the buttons. Basil had stopped leaving messages on her voicemail these days. But he texted a lot. Mostly she managed to zap them unread. But today she saw one she had thought was from her limousine service.

As soon as she saw it was not, she killed it. But not soon enough.

The message was the same as always. The words changed. But the theme was constant.

U R MYN.

CHAPTER TWO

JEMIMA let herself into the apartment. It was dark and silent.
She dropped her overnight bag and closed the door.

'Pepper?' she called, without much hope.

But there was no answer. Well, it was only what she had
expected. Izzy was away in the ice fields, helping her love
with his training. She had hoped that her cousin might be
here, though.

Jemima hefted the bag over her shoulder. Switching on
lights, she made her way to the kitchen.

It was the heart of their shared home. Here they sat at the
table and laughed and argued and made plans. Now it was
unnaturally tidy. No flowers on the table. No scribbled messages on the memory board. All the work surfaces were
clear and gleaming. Even the answering machine was neatly
aligned in the corner, with what looked like a week's post
in front of it. The last person in here had clearly been the
cleaning lady.

Jemima shivered and dropped her trim flight bag. She
flicked on the radio and bopped gently to the music as she
opened the fridge.

Lots of water. A couple of bottles of wine. Some elderly
cheese. It didn't look as if Pepper had been here for days.

'With her Steven in Oxford,' said Jemima aloud.

Just like Izzy, with her Dominic.

'And I could be out on the town with Francis Hale-
Smith,' she mocked herself. 'Holding hands whenever we
spotted a camera.'

It was even more chilling than the empty flat.

She started to make coffee, although she didn't really
want it, and hacked off a small corner of the dying cheese.

Not because she wanted that either, but because Izzy always made her some food when she came in late. Or she'd always used to.

'Hi, Jay Jay. How was Paris? And how have you been?' she said to the empty chair.

She walked round to the other side of the table and answered herself. 'Oh, you know—busy, busy. And my ex-manager won't leave me alone. Hounding me seems to be his new career choice. He's really putting his back into it, twenty-four-seven.'

In the silence she did not sound anything like as ironic as she'd meant to.

'Damn!' Her voice broke at last.

She sank down on a kitchen chair and dropped her head in her hands.

The phone started to ring. She ignored it. She had not cried, not once, since Basil started his campaign. And now it didn't seem as if she could stop. She didn't even try to answer the phone.

The answering programme clicked onto Izzy's voice. She sounded as if she were laughing.

'We can't take your call at the moment. But talk nicely and we might get back to you. Here come the beeps.'

Jemima gave an audible hiccup. They had laughed so much when Izzy recorded that. It had been airlessly hot. All the windows open. They'd been drinking white wine spritzers and they had juggled ice cubes to decide who got to record the message. Izzy had been wearing a tee shirt and nothing else, and she said you could hear it in her voice on the recording.

Now Jemima reached across and pressed the outgoing message button, just to remind herself of that night. Now Izzy had Dom, and Pepper was getting married. And Jemima?

Jemima had her very own stalker, she thought with savage irony.

She gave herself a mental shake. This was stupid.

Besides, she hated being so sorry for herself. It made her feel a wimp.

She stood up, looking for kitchen roll to blot her streaming eyes.

And again the phone burst into shrill life.

She jumped so hard that she knocked over the kitchen roll. While she was retrieving it the answering programme kicked in. Izzy's lovely laughing voice, and then...

'Welcome home, Jemima,' said a voice she knew.

She stopped dead. Her hand stilled on the paper roll. Suddenly the self-pitying eyes were dry. Dry as her mouth.

'Pick up. I know you're there.'

Slowly she straightened and put the kitchen roll back on the fitment very precisely. Her throat hurt. She swallowed, looking at the telephone. She did not move.

The voice got impatient. 'Come on, pick up. Don't be stupid. I saw you put the lights on.'

Could he see her? The kitchen window was three feet away. Slowly Jemima backed to the door and out into the windowless corridor. She could hear her own breathing.

The voice pursued her. 'Pick up, Jemima. We need to talk. You know we do. Come on, pick up. You owe me that.' It sounded so reasonable, put like that.

Only she knew it wasn't reasonable. And neither was Basil any more.

She backed up against the wall. Her hands were slippery with sweat.

Think! she told herself.

'I bloody *made* you, you bitch,' he spat, fury overcoming that spurious reason at last.

Jemima blocked it out.

He must have been waiting outside, she thought feverishly. Or he might have followed her. She hadn't seen him when she'd left her interview with Madame. But then half the time she didn't see him. He would just step out of the crowd, smiling except for those mad, angry eyes.

And he would say...

He would say...

'You are mine.'

Just as he was saying it now.

The flat had never felt so empty. Jemima looked round and took a decision.

I have got to get out of here.

It was actually surprisingly easy. She had a ticket for New York in her bag which she didn't need any more. And one of the great things about first class air tickets is that they are as transferable as it gets.

All she had to do was get out of the building without the watcher following her. What she needed was a veil, thought Jemima dryly. Or, failing that, a crash helmet.

A crash helmet...

The pizza delivery guy was so intrigued he would probably have lent her his helmet and jacket anyway. But the fistful of notes certainly helped. She parked his bike in front of the all-night pharmacy and waited to hand over the key. She called a cab while she was waiting. It arrived as he came strolling down the road.

'Thanks,' she said.

'Hey, no sweat. Pleased I could help.'

She had told him it was boyfriend trouble. Clearly dazzled, he had not doubted her for a moment. It was going to be all round the pub this weekend, thought Jemima.

She did not care. She gave him a quick kiss on the cheek. 'My hero.'

He beamed. And held the door of the taxi cab open for her with a gallant flourish.

'Good luck.'

'Thank you,' said Jemima with feeling. 'I can do with it. I really can.'

And she could. Change the flight? The booking clerk was helpfulness personified. Yes, certainly, no problem. Where did she want to go?

'Ah.'

For a moment Jemima's mind went completely blank. Wildly, she scanned the posters behind the desk. They all looked like the sort of photographs she was used to starring in, only without the high fashion.

She shrugged. Oh, well, if you'd been everywhere, what else could you expect? This was an escape, after all, not a proper holiday.

She played the eeny-meeny game in her head, and it landed on silver sand and palm trees beside an improbably jade sea.

She nodded to the poster. 'There.'

'The Caribbean? Yes, madam. Which island?'

On the point of saying she didn't care, Jemima stopped. From somewhere out of the well of memory a name surfaced.

'Is there somewhere called Pentecost Island?' The moment she said it she felt a tingle, as if this was somehow meant. She stood up straighter. 'Do you go there?'

The clerk smiled. 'We can get you there, Ms Dare. Via Barbados. First class again?'

And that was how easy it was.

No one in the world would know where she was. So not even Basil could bribe or bully or spy on anyone to tell him.

Alone in the bathroom in the first class lounge, Jemima studied herself in the mirror as narrowly as Basil had used to study her. She looked fine. Tired under the harsh lighting, but as well as anyone else would look on this overnight flight. She had beaten Basil!

'Gotcha!' she said, punching the air.

She almost skipped onto to the plane.

Her euphoria lasted through the night, through the long, dull early-morning wait at Barbados airport, through the trip on the far from first class local island hopper. It lasted right up to the moment she disembarked at Pentecost.

The airport was small. Shiny and modern, and clean as a new machine, but tiny. Jemima had never seen an airport like it. Once through passport control, she found a concourse that would just about take a row of plastic chairs and a small coffee stall.

She stared round blankly.

'Toy Town Airport,' she said aloud.

The coffee stall boasted a steaming urn and some delicious slices of home-made cake. And a friendly woman as wide as the stall.

'We're not a big place,' she agreed.

Jemima jumped and blushed. Damn, she had got to stop talking to herself. 'Oh, I'm sorry. I didn't mean—'

But the woman was not in the least offended. 'Small and proud of it,' she beamed, serving Jemima with a generous wodge of banana bread.

Jemima bit into it with pleasure. She had been too tired to eat on the plane. This warm spicy-smelling stuff was ambrosial.

'I guess I've got used to airport malls,' she said ruefully, licking her fingers. 'Oh, well, I'll have to go shopping in town. But there must be a tourist desk somewhere around?'

The woman shook her head placidly. 'No call for it. The tourists all know where they're going before they get to Pentecost.'

'Oh.'

The friendly coffee-seller looked Jemima up and down assessingly. Jemima could have groaned aloud. She knew what the woman was seeing and it wasn't very impressive: the cheap jeans had been a great disguise when she'd wanted to look like a pizza delivery person, but they hadn't survived the flights too well. And the tee shirt, with its glitter logo that had been amusing in metropolitan London, now looked simply slutty. Add to that a too tired, too pale face, and red hair scragged back in two disintegrating plaits and you had a pretty unimpressive picture. Not a desirable import at all, thought Jemima wryly.

She had forgotten her luggage. The little island hopper planes didn't have any seating differential, but the gold and

silver identity label on her swag bag gave her away. It just
screamed 'First class'.

The woman's eyes lingered on it. She gave a small nod.
'You'll be for Pirate's Point.'

Jemima followed her eyes and looked down at the label.
'W-will I?'

The woman waved a hand at one of the few posters on
the single advertising hoarding. And there it was, sand-
wiched between a notice about prohibited foodstuffs and an
out-of-date cinema schedule, a photograph she recognised.
Turquoise sea, palm trees, surf topped with white like soft
meringue.

It clicked into place like the last piece of a jigsaw.

Abby's friend! The mysterious N, who had sent her a
postcard but wasn't a danger to her marriage because he had
known her when she wore braces on her teeth. *That* was
where Jemima had heard of Pentecost Island before.

Pirate's Point Casino. All the holiday you'll ever need.

Jemima went over to look at it.

'"Luxury development, gardens, beaches, international
cuisine. And the chance to win your fortune. Everything you
need in one complex,"' she read.

It sounded exactly what Jemima would have paid good
money to avoid. She turned back to the coffee-seller.

'Well, I was hoping to stay in town. See a bit of local
life,' she said tactfully. 'Would it be difficult to get a room?'

The woman shook her head decisively. 'All town places
fill up this time of year.'

Jemima's heart sank.

'You talk to Mr Derringer out at Pirate's Point,' the
woman said comfortably. 'He'll take you in. Big place like
that, with the casino and all, they bound to have a room.'

Jemima smiled wryly. The casino! That was hardly the
escape she had imagined. A load of tired New Yorkers, who
didn't like the desert or the weather in Atlantic City, playing
slot machines.

'A casino is not quite what I had in mind...'

A trolley of medical supplies and baby powder rolled out from the customs area. The man in charge of it applied the brakes and leaned his arm on top of the boxes.

'There's the place in town,' he offered.

'That's for those kids who crew on the boats,' said the coffee-seller loftily. 'Not a young lady.' And her eyes skimmed the silver and gold label again.

He was less impressed by the first-class trappings. 'Well, now, that may be true. But beggars can't be choosers.'

The woman was not listening. She was looking over Jemima's shoulder, and a big grin grew from ear to ear.

'You lucky. Here's the man to help you,' she said. 'Hi, Niall.'

Behind them, an unmistakably English voice said lazily, 'Hi, Violet. How's it going?'

English!

Basil!

Jemima spun round, heart thundering so hard she felt that it would tear her in two.

She half threw her bag away, ready to defend herself. Basil had once seized her arm and held it agonisingly high behind her back until she had agreed to do some stunt that he was insisting on. Logically, she did not think he would do that again in public. But logic did not have much to do with her feelings about Basil. She took a step back, half turning away, gathering herself to fight back...

But it wasn't Basil. It was a man she hadn't seen before.

If she had seen him she wouldn't have forgotten him.

He was tall, with a lazy grin and denim shorts that looked as if they were probably illegal. Apart from the shorts he was wearing nothing but some disgraceful flip-flops and a tan that the male models she knew would kill for. But it was not the spectacular tan or even the outrageous gear that hit her between the eyes. It was his face.

This was a face that would stick in the memory. Not because he was particularly handsome. He wasn't. His nose was crooked and much too big, and the high, haughty cheekbones were far too prominent. But it had intensity and a fierce intelligence. Oh, yes, definitely unforgettable.

And just now his eyebrows were as high as they could go.

'Hey, up,' he said. 'Oh, boy, have you got a bad conscience.'

Jemima stared at him, bemused. 'What?'

'You look as if you think you're going to be arrested,' said Haughty Cheekbones. 'Put your bag down. Look. No handcuffs.' He sounded amused.

Jemima lowered her bag, feeling rather a fool. It irritated her profoundly. But, for all that, he still took her breath away. He looked like one of those Renaissance princes. Probably one who had people locked up on the whim of the moment, she thought, hanging on to her irritation for all she was worth.

In fact, that was why you wouldn't forget that face, thought Jemima, trying her calm her galloping pulse. It was too much of everything—too dark, too shuttered, too impatient. And—she looked for the first time at the wide, sensual mouth and swallowed hard—much, much too passionate.

Violet of the coffee stall could clearly take all that passion in her stride.

'We fine,' she interceded placidly. 'But lady here just got off the plane. Nowhere to stay.' She patted Jemima proprietorially on the shoulder. 'You take her back to Al's place.'

Jemima's pulse had returned to normal. Well, nearly. But this sounded as if Violet was sending her off to the slave market.

'Al's place?' she echoed.

The Renaissance prince cast her a sardonic glance and she felt her cheeks heat. Damn, did the man read minds as well?

'Local name,' said Violet carelessly, all but ignoring Jemima in her determination to convince Haughty Cheekbones. 'You going to take her back with you?'

He clearly didn't like it. That voluptuous mouth tightened. 'You're a fixer, Violet.' He didn't say anything to
Jemima at all.

Jemima found her voice. Now she saw he wasn't Basil
she wasn't afraid of him, she told herself fiercely. Passionate
or not, he was just a man—and a stranger. She could handle
strangers. Even relaxed, nearly naked strangers, with hair-
roughened chests and a mean streak.

'No need,' she said crisply, avoiding his eyes. 'I came on
spec and it clearly wasn't a good idea. I'll just stay here and
take the next plane out.'

'Can't do that,' said the Englishman, relaxed to the point
of boredom. 'There isn't another flight until tomorrow.'

Damned Toy Town island, fumed Jemima silently. Aloud,
she said brightly, 'Then I'll find somewhere to stay in town.'

He shrugged. 'Fat chance. There are only three hotels,
and they'll all be full if you haven't booked.'

She met his eyes. He looked back with total indifference.

Jemima told herself that she wasn't vain and she didn't
expect every man in the world to fall at her feet. But it was
a long time since a man had looked at her with such total
absence of interest. At her? Through her! It made her feel
cold and just a little afraid.

I'm never going to be afraid of a man again.

It was all she needed to put some steel into her backbone.
She stuck up her chin and said, with a very good imitation
of friendliness, 'Then I won't waste my time. I'll sleep
here.'

'In the airport?' Even Mr Indifference was taken aback.

'Yes.'

'Do that a lot, do you?'

Actually, she had never done it before. But her sister was
an experienced traveller, and Jemima had been listening to
Izzy's stories of missed connections and jaunty improvisa-
tion all her life. In comparison with Izzy's hair-raising experiences, sleeping in a clean and peaceful airport didn't

seem too difficult. Even for a spoilt model girl, thought Jemima dryly.

She tilted her chin. 'You got a problem with that?'

He shrugged again. 'Not me. But they have a strong vagrancy law here. They'll probably throw you in jail.'

Jemima tried to stay cool, but her assumed friendliness slipped a bit.

'Then that will solve the problem of where I spend the night, won't it?' she said sweetly.

Too sweetly. This time when he looked at her it was not with indifference. It was with undisguised temper.

She glared back.

Reluctantly, it seemed, his lips twitched. 'Okay, you've made your point.' Suddenly, there was an unexpected undertone of laughter. 'You don't want to go to Al's. I see that. But I don't think you've got an alternative, at least for tonight. Tell her, Violet.'

The coffee-seller nodded vigorously. 'Listen to the man.'

'So neither of us has much choice,' said the Englishman dispassionately. 'I'll give you a lift out to Pirate's Point. Al will give you a room for the night. You can get a taxi back tomorrow morning and take the first flight out. How's that for compromise?'

Jemima bowed to the inevitable. It didn't make her like him any more.

'Oh—okay, then.'

His dark eyes glinted with real amusement. 'No need to go overboard with the gratitude,' he said dryly.

It was a rebuke. Jemima did not like that either.

'Thank you,' she said between her teeth.

'You're welcome.'

He turned away. 'Violet, have you seen—?'

But at that moment the doors to the arrivals area opened again and a tall black man in a startling white uniform came through. He came over, smiling widely.

'Hi, Niall. Al conned you into coming to pick the stuff

up, did he? We were waiting for him at the gates. You got the pick-up?'

Niall shook his head. 'The Range Rover.'

'Oh, well, bring it round. We got three pallets to load.'

Niall said to Jemima, 'Where's your stuff?'

She gestured at the swag bag, sitting squashily in front of the coffee stall.

His eyebrows flew up. 'That all?'

'Yes,' she said, bristling.

'You travel light!'

Her hackles rose. 'Hey, what do you need for a holiday in the Caribbean?'

She repressed the thought that all the gear she had was for Europe in February. She had intended to pick up a bikini and some shorts at the airport. But she was not admitting that to Haughty Cheekbones.

The Englishman looked sardonic. 'A hotel room would have been good. Or do you make a habit of sleeping where you fall?'

On the brink of denying it, Jemima caught herself. It was the perfect alibi, after all. Just in case Basil did, by some fluke, manage to track her to Pentecost. She could let everyone think she was a student backpacker, floating from island to island. So if Basil turned up asking for an international model they could all say, On Pentecost? Nah!

So she tilted her head back to meet his disparaging glance.

'I go where the wind blows me,' she said naughtily. 'Does that worry you?'

For a moment his eyes were as dark and fierce as any Renaissance potentate offended by a minion. Then he seemed to remember who and where he was. He gave a crack of laughter.

'You really know how to get under a man's skin, don't you?' he said ruefully. 'How you live is nothing to do with me, thank God. Come along, then, wind-rider. Let's get you stashed before I start loading.' He whipped her bag off the

floor and onto his shoulder as if it weighed nothing and
raised a hand to the coffee stall. 'See you, Violet.'

'You'll like Pirate's Point,' Violet told Jemima. 'Enjoy.'
And, to him, 'Bye, Niall. Come back soon.'

The two men strode ahead out of the main doors, talking.
Ignored, Jemima set her teeth and followed.

Outside the air-conditioned building the hot, still air was
like walking into a wall of toasted marshmallow. It also
smelled of plane fuel. Jemima stopped dead, gagging.

The man called Niall stopped, looking over his shoulder.
'You okay?'

'I'm fine.'

And she was. After the icy rain of London, the heat
seemed to reach out and hug her. She drew a deep, deep
breath and caught up with him as the man in uniform peeled
off towards some high steel gates.

Niall opened the passenger door of a big Range Rover
and tossed her bag up into it.

'You'll have to sit with your feet on it,' he said practically. 'The back seat is reserved for loo rolls and coffee this
trip.'

He adjusted the back seats to lie flat while Jemima scrambled up into the vehicle. Then he swung round into the
driver's seat and set the thing in drive just as the gates began
to swing open. He drove, she saw, with more precision than
one would expect from his careless manner. He shot the
vehicle through the gates before they were even half open
and not a scrap of paint was scratched. Then he parked
meticulously beside the waiting boxes.

'You're good at this, aren't you?' she said involuntarily.

'Running errands and an unlicensed taxi service?' he
mocked. 'Oh, sure.'

She looked at the small tower of goods. 'Can I help?'

'Load up, you mean? No, thanks. I do better on my own.
Get my own rhythm going.' He gave her a sudden smile.
He was startlingly sexy when he smiled. A Renaissance

prince eyeing up a possible favourite. 'But thanks for the offer.'

He got out of the vehicle. Just as well. Jemima could feel the heat in her face all over again. She took herself firmly to task, watching as he started to load up rapidly.

He was right, she thought. He *did* do better than he would have done with her amateur assistance. He was very fast, not a movement wasted.

She frowned. The semi-naked beach bum and the precision driver with a scientific loading method did not seem to sit together very comfortably. Was he hiding something?

At once she laughed at herself. *Just because you're on the run, that doesn't mean everyone in the world has a secret!*

But, even so, as she watched the muscles in his arms bunch and release, bunch and release, she thought, *He doesn't try to look like a muscle man, but there's a lot of latent power there. I wouldn't like to cross him.*

Now, that really was ludicrous. Especially as she had already promised herself that she was never going to be afraid of a man again. Far better to stop fantasising about that surprising strength and concentrate on what she was going to call herself. If she was serious about leaving supermodel Jemima Dare in her box for a week, she'd better think up a name and fast.

It was not until they were belting down a stretch of newly surfaced road that he said, 'You'd better tell me your name. I'm Niall.'

'So I gathered,' said Jemima, a touch acidly. And went on, without so much as an infinitesimal pause, 'Jay Jay Cooper.'

It would have passed any lie detector test, she thought complacently. Cooper was her mother's name. Jay Jay was what the family called her.

He nodded gravely. 'Welcome to Pentecost, Jay Jay. Have you been in the Caribbean long?'

Jemima thought about the last time, in November. It had

been a shoot for the Belinda project. They had all put up at a palatial villa on a private island. She had had a mountain of luggage, had never emerged from her suite without a full hair and make-up job, and had given interviews to the international gossip journalists every spare moment when she wasn't actually working on the shoot.

She bit back a smile. 'Off and on,' she said airily.

'Work or pleasure?'

'This time it's pleasure.'

He nodded. 'So what do you do when you're not bumming around on pleasure trips?'

She hadn't prepared for that one and had to think quickly. 'Nothing very interesting. Bit of this. Bit of that.'

He sent her a look that was part mockery, part suspicion. 'What sort of this and that?'

'Oh, I've waitressed,' she said truthfully. Well, she had—when she was at school.

It was not enough. He was still waiting.

She thought wildly and borrowed from Izzy's chequered career yet again. 'Cruise ship hospitality. Typing and filing. Anything that pays the rent, basically.'

'All to fund your travel habit?'

'I suppose so.'

He nodded. 'Me too.'

'What?'

This time the look he gave he was different. Slower. Deeper. Also more thoughtful. Appraising, somehow. As if he was taking her in properly at last. And not trusting her an inch.

Jemima shifted in her seat, suddenly uneasy. He could not have disturbed her more if he had actually reached out and touched her.

But all he said was, 'I'm a natural-born hobo too.'

She bridled at the *too*. Then reminded herself that was what she wanted him to think. Or did she? She couldn't really care less what a beach bum thought about her, could she?

She was still pondering that one when he said, 'I've been travelling the world for over fifteen years now. We've probably been to some of the same places.'

That brought her up sharp.

'Um—probably,' said Jemima in a hollow voice.

'We must compare notes.'

'Er—yes.'

'Tonight, say? We're going to be eating in the same place, after all. Why don't I see you in the bar and we can eat together?'

'Great.' Jemima's enthusiasm was so forced that it was amazing he did not notice it, she thought.

But he didn't. 'It's a date,' he said cheerfully.

Jemima could have screamed. So much for lying low and being her own woman! She had not been on this Toy Town island for more than a couple of hours and already she'd got a date she didn't want with a man she didn't like. A man, moreover, who had the hard, dissecting look of a Renaissance ruler who wouldn't brook being lied to. Tonight, she thought furiously, was going to be hard work.

She stared straight ahead at the road shimmering in the heat and told herself she had to do better than this tomorrow. But for tonight she would just have to busk it. She could do that, surely? Just for one night.

'Seven okay for you?'

She drew a deep breath. Go on, perform, she told herself. That's what models do, for heaven's sake. And you do a great performance. Francis Hale-Smith was saying so only yesterday.

He sent her another of those deep, disturbing looks. Jemima felt her skin prickle with awareness. She could feel him willing her to look at him. It was like a physical tug of war to resist it.

Smile for the camera.

She swallowed and forced herself to say, 'I look forward to it.' She had to brace herself physically to get it out.

He smiled. Even not looking at him, Jemima knew that it was an ambiguous smile. It made her feel hot all over, not just her face this time.

'Not as much as I do,' he said softly.

CHAPTER THREE

PIRATE'S POINT was a surprise. She had been braced for concrete monstrosities dwarfing the beach and Nevada-style neon.

'But it's beautiful,' said Jemima, sitting up sharply in surprise.

'Al will be overwhelmed,' murmured Niall.

The bay was a great semicircle, fringed by a beach of ivory sand. The hotel was everything that the poster had promised: three-storey blocks set among gardens that had been planted to jungle density. But as the drive curved down the hill towards the sea Jemima found she could never see more than one block of apartments at any one time. Even the casino, visible from the road, right out on the promontory that formed the most westerly point of the beach, looked like a Spanish hacienda, set among palm trees and hibiscus. Not a neon sign in sight.

'Phew,' she said. 'No flashing lights.'

He chuckled. 'Gambling is not all burgers and slot machines. You put a casino in a place like this, you're selling a lifestyle.'

Niall did not look at her. But even the set of his shoulders was mocking. Jemima's eyes narrowed.

'Are you an expert on gambling?' There was a distinct edge to her voice.

His mouth tilted in a private smile. 'You could put it like that.'

Jemima knew she was being laughed at. But as she did not know why she didn't have a clue how to deal with it. She ground her teeth.

'I don't gamble,' she announced.

He gave a great shout of laughter.

Jemima could have screamed with fury. But she was honest enough to admit—well, to herself—that she deserved his mockery. Her remark had been meant as a put-down. But as soon as she'd said it she had realised how impossibly smug it sounded. Smug and prim and all the things she was pretending not to be. All the things she *wasn't*.

And it was all Haughty Cheekbones's fault.

'Do you enjoy winding people up?' she said frostily.

He glanced sideways, still chuckling. 'Can't get enough of it.'

Jemima made a noise which, even to herself, sounded like 'Grrrr,' and turned her shoulder, looking pointedly out at the landscape.

He was taking the Range Rover along a swirling drive between dense bushes and vine-covered hotel buildings. The sea appeared and disappeared with the turns in the road. In the afternoon sun it gleamed like the coat of a sleepy tiger.

Jemima forgot that she had made a prune of herself and Niall Whoever-He-Was had laughed at her. This was just too beautiful.

She swung round to watch the sea slip away behind a wall that was covered with bougainvillaea so purple it hurt the eyes. 'This is amazing,' she said, awed. 'Once you're down off the road you can't see one block from any of the others.'

'Try not to sound so surprised when you meet Al and Ellie,' advised Niall dryly. 'They've worked hard at this place. They're proud of it.'

But when they arrived at the porticoed entrance Jemima had no time to congratulate the manager on the sympathetic landscaping of his hotel complex. Or anything else. A small, fierce woman was waiting for them, tapping her foot. She ignored Jemima completely and launched into a tirade.

'There you are, Niall. What on earth kept you? The kitchen has run out of everything. Everything. We're nearly an hour late starting dinner. Do you realise that?'

He grinned. 'Sorry, Ellie. Picked up some excess baggage.'

The small woman nodded to Jemima without interest and shot past them. She dived into the back of the Range Rover and began to scrabble like an oversized hamster.

Niall gestured to the jeans-clad bottom which was all they could see of her.

'Ellie, your hostess,' he said, grinning. 'I'll do the other half of the introduction later. And here is Al, who will find you a room.'

Al was a lot less fierce.

'A room, sure,' he said easily. 'Are you a diver or a gambler?'

'Neither,' said Jemima, taken aback. 'Is it part of the entry requirement?'

'Our guests are usually one or the other.'

And when she still looked puzzled Niall said blandly, 'It makes a difference to which rooms Al gives them.'

'What?'

'Divers get up early. Gamblers go to bed late. Al separates them so they don't disturb each other.'

'How er—efficient,' said Jemima.

Al was not as attractive as Niall, but his smile was a great deal kinder. 'We've found it works.'

Leaving Ellie to excavate the provisions she wanted, Al took Jemima's squashy bag and led the way to the cool stone lobby. Old-fashioned ceiling fans whirred and small palms stood about in great brass tubs. There was Cole Porter on the sound system. But the place was empty. Al went to a big desk in the corner and sat down at a computer.

His fingers flickered and Jemima saw a screen come up. 'So, who do you want to sleep with?' he asked cheerfully.

Niall gave a sound that was suspiciously like a choke.

Al looked up at him grinning. 'Niall's a gambler,' he said, as if the information would be helpful.

Jemima had a nasty feeling of male solidarity ranged against her. She refused to give them the satisfaction of acknowledging it. Instead she smiled sweetly back into Al's teasing grin, and completely ignored Niall's artificial stone face.

'So he said,' she agreed without expression.

'And she's not,' offered Niall, suspiciously bland.

Al's eyebrows rose.

Jemima said hastily, 'I'm a lark, not an owl. Better put me with the diving party.'

Al pushed a registration card across the desk. Jemima picked up the pen and bent over it. And as she did so she caught the look that passed between him and Niall. No doubt at all. Pure masculine amusement.

Jemima's head reared up with indignation. Men did not laugh at her. They looked at her with longing—or lust—or utter hopeless yearning. She whipped round, glaring.

And found that Niall had stepped forward and they were unexpectedly close. Too close. Almost touching.

At once Niall had his face under control.

Jemima thought suddenly, He's done this before. He's used to hiding his thoughts at a moment's notice.

He was good at it too. All desire to shout left her abruptly. She took a slow step backwards.

His eyes darkened, and just for a moment she thought she could detect what he was thinking. She saw puzzlement. Then surprise. Then his head went back as if he knew she could see through the mask. And then she saw the naked flare of desire, urgent and unmistakable.

They stared at each other, speechless.

A delicious shiver rippled up her spine. *Careful, Jemima. That would not be a good idea.*

She put the pen down and moved out of touching range.

'And your credit card?' said Al, busy with her registration, not noticing.

Niall and Jemima looked at each other like conspirators.

As if in a dream, Jemima handed her card across. Then realised, too late, that it had her real name on it. She tensed.

But Al did not comment. 'Sign here.'

He checked her signature and gave the credit card back to her.

Jemima relaxed. Of course, hoteliers must be used to women turning up with papers in other names—divorced women, remarried women. Hoteliers would have to be discreet.

Al passed a strip of plastic through a machine and handed it across the desk. 'Room 409. It will have to be a quick tour now,' he said apologetically. 'We've got a cruise party in for dinner.'

Niall said easily, 'I'll show Jay Jay to her room, if you like.'

All signs of that flaring desire had gone and he was laughing again. Jemima told herself that she was relieved.

Al pulled a face, then gave a rueful smile. 'Sorry about this,' he said to Jemima. 'We don't usually co-opt guests. But it's just gone mad today.'

Jemima glanced at Niall, frowning. 'A guest?'

She could not believe it. This too competent pirate in his barely decent shorts? A guest? Here?

'Yes, Al lets me stay here,' he told her solemnly. 'I clean up okay.'

Jemima felt herself redden. His face was bland but she knew that he was laughing at her. Again!

'I'm sure you do,' she said with restraint. 'I could do with a clean-up myself. If you're going to be a boy scout, I'd be really glad to see my room now.'

'Sure. Come with me.'

He went to take her bag from Al, but Jemima got there first. She felt she had something to prove, though she was not quite sure what. She seized the bag and looped it over her shoulder, clamping it protectively to her side.

'See you at dinner,' Al called after them. This time he did not bother to suppress his grin.

Jemima pretended not to notice.

Niall took her to her room via a briskly effective orientation walk.

'Bar.' He waved a hand at the wicker-roofed area on the beach. 'See you there later. Garden dining area.' He waved inland. 'We can eat inside if the wind gets up. Pool. There's another one further up the hill, near my cottage. Colder, but not chlorinated. Your block.'

He stood back to let her precede him onto the steps that led up to an open walkway among the trees.

'Your cottage?' said Jemima puzzled. 'You mean you don't stay with the gamblers after all?'

'They have three or four cottages in the grounds. I prefer one of those,' said Niall. 'More private.'

Again Jemima felt that little shiver of unacknowledged awareness. She was not going to ask about why he wanted extra privacy. She was not even going to think about it. She was *not*.

'But the apartments are fine,' he said reassuringly. 'You'll see. Your terrace comes with damn great potted banana plants. And the electricity is a lot more reliable.' He ran lightly up the exposed stairs onto an open-air landing that was brushed by huge leaves. 'The light switch is here.' He showed her.

'Thank you,' said Jemima, panting slowly after him up the stairs. She was cursing her pride. The swag bag weighed a ton after one flight.

He looked down at her and laughed. Then, relenting, he reached out a negligent hand and just lifted it off her shoulder as if it were a toddler's lunch box.

Jemima straightened, glaring.

He ignored her, running lightly up the remaining flight to the top gangway, and made his way to the door at the end. He inserted the card and Jemima heard the click as it unlocked.

'I hate these things,' Niall said conversationally. 'All you need is a good power cut and you can't get in.' He flung the door open with a flourish.

'Or out,' said Jemima, refusing to pant any more.

'That wouldn't necessarily be so bad,' murmured Niall. 'In some circumstances, anyway.'

His admiring look was pantomime. Nothing to do with that flare of pure flame at the desk.

She gave him a withering look. 'Forget it. I don't rise to schoolboy innuendo.'

He laughed aloud. 'Shame.'

'And if I get locked in by a power cut I shall climb down a drainpipe.'

'I just bet you would too,' he agreed, his eyes dancing.

She mistrusted the dancing eyes even more than she resented his horribly superior fitness. 'Believe it,' she said grimly.

He flung up his hands. 'Okay. I won't give you a guided tour of the bedroom or the romantic terrace. Just the basics—' He went swiftly round the apartment, pointing things out. 'Air-conditioning unit. Umbrella—the rain here doesn't last long, but it's hard. Candles in case the light goes out. Torch. Al has just put in ankle-lights along the paths, but people like to wander off on their own to look at the stars.' He unearthed a black rubber torch that looked like an offensive weapon and patted it kindly. 'Don't go without this. And don't forget—night falls fast here.'

'Thank you,' said Jemima, with restraint.

He was not deceived. 'Oh, but I don't have to tell you that, do I? You're a seasoned traveller.'

She gave him a sweet, angry smile. 'But it's so nice to be told what to do in case I forget. I just love a man to be protective.'

He pursed his lips in a silent whistle. 'Ouch. Were those toes I just trod on?'

Jemima was angry with herself. Sure, the man was annoying, with his assumption of superiority. But he was not Basil, telling her what to do with her every moment and threatening to hurt her if she didn't follow his instructions to the letter.

She turned away, biting her lip. 'I don't know what you mean.' It was a lie.

'What I mean,' said Niall calmly, 'is that you have an attitude problem.'

Jemima gasped and whipped round in outrage. It was one thing to know you had over-reacted. It was another to be crunched by a half-naked beach bum. Guest or no guest!

She drew herself up to her considerable height. 'Excuse me?'

'Fascinating.'

He was, she found, actually having the gall to stare at her as if she were some new species he hadn't come across before.

'Goodbye,' she said.

'You don't mean that.'

'*Goodbye.*'

'But I haven't shown you—'

'Whatever it is, I'll find it for myself, thank you.'

She walked towards him purposefully. To her relief, he backed off. She hadn't been sure he would go like a gentleman.

'You make it very difficult for a chap to be neighbourly.'

'Thank you. I appreciate it,' said Jemima, still walking. 'Goodbye.'

He retreated to the doorway. 'Not goodbye. *Au revoir.*'

She stopped, disconcerted.

'What?'

The wide, sensual mouth curved into a grin of pure satisfaction.

'We have a date,' he reminded her gently. 'Don't forget. Or I'll have to come and get you.'

He sauntered out before she could answer.

The moment the door closed behind him Niall stopped sauntering. He made it back to the reception desk in record time. Al looked up, surprised.

'Dinner, Al. I need a private table tonight,' Niall said crisply.

A grin dawned. 'Romancing the feisty Ms Cooper?'

Niall narrowed his eyes at him. 'I'd be very surprised if her name is really Cooper. Or if there is a word of truth in anything else she said. Show me the register card.'

'Wow,' said Al, grin unabated. 'She's made a real impact, hasn't she?'

Niall was irritated. 'She's a manipulator. I had several stepmothers. I recognise the signs.' He snapped his fingers. 'Card, please.'

'You want to have dinner with her because she reminds you of your stepmothers?' Al was frankly incredulous.

Niall shrugged and leaned over the desk to whisk the card off Al's pile of filing. He scanned it, frowning.

'Of course not,' he said absently.

'So you do fancy her?'

Niall looked mulish. 'Jemima Jane Dare,' he mused, committing it to memory. 'Jemima Jane, I'm going to find out what your game is.'

Al shook his head, puzzled. 'Why bother?'

Niall hesitated at that. At last he showed his teeth. 'I don't like being manipulated.'

Al gave a sigh and abandoned any attempt to understand his old friend. 'It's your life,' he said. 'Table for two on the terrace, then. I'll tell Ellie.'

Jemima did not even unpack. She just collapsed on a bed big enough for a family of six and fell into a deep, dreamless sleep.

When she awoke it was dark. For a moment she was disorientated. The window was in the wrong place, the light switch wasn't where she expected, the place smelled wrong... And then she came fully awake and, as she always did, remembered the next problem she had to wrestle with.

She had dealt with Basil. She had escaped.

Only to fall into the arms of Niall the beach bum.

Jemima sat bolt upright at the thought. The last vestiges of sleep fled. She groped for light and the time.

Nearly seven. Well, she would have to be late.

'Woman's privilege,' she said, scrambling across the bed and reaching for her sponge bag.

Only—she didn't want to feel like a woman with Niall the beach bum. Not in the smallest, most superficial particular. She didn't want any acknowledgement of her femininity at all. No special concession to a pretty girl. No doors opened or chairs held. Above all, no flirting. When she walked away from Niall the beach bum she wanted to leave him with the memory of a plain, sexless traveller whom he would never think of again.

'You can do it,' she told herself.

But it didn't take cosmetics and styling to make Jemima Dare a stunner. All it took was a rapid shower. Inevitably the grime of the journey washed out of her hair, leaving it a feathery cloud of red and gold and vermilion and bronze. Even skewered ruthlessly on top of her head, it still glowed. Soft with its recent washing, it seemed determined to descend, too.

'Blast, blast, blast,' muttered Jemima, stabbing another maxi-pin into her head so hard that she winced.

Looking in the mirror without vanity, she knew that plain and sexless was not really an option.

Oh, well, she would just have to be seriously nasty to him. That should put him off. She didn't think that Niall the beach bum was lining up to join her fan club anyway. So it shouldn't be that hard.

Although there had been that spark at the airport. And when their eyes had locked in that odd moment of naked desire. But—

'It takes two to spark,' said Jemima aloud, with great firmness.

At the airport she had not been expecting it. Nor at the hotel desk. Now that she was warned she would be on her guard. Definitely no sparks!

*   *   *

But she almost lost that one at first sight.

She was half an hour late. The beachside bar was filling up. Under a palm tree a man was murmuring dreamy Latin American love songs to an acoustic guitar. There was a low buzz of conversation.

It was a mixed bunch. There were men in elegant blazers, men in scruffy tee shirts, and everything in between. There was even one man, with his back to her, in the full Oscar Awards tuxedo. As for the women—Jemima's expert eye told her that none of them was wearing the latest designer gear but several were very well dressed indeed. And one or two of the older women had spectacular jewellery.

There was a lot of quiet money around here, she thought. It would be interesting to see how Niall the beach bum managed to fit in. She glanced round the bar again.

Then the man in the tuxedo turned round. And Jemima saw exactly how Niall fitted in.

The black tailored jacket should have made him look tamed, less powerful. It did the reverse. The raw physicality was in hiding, not extinguished. And Jemima knew—*how* she knew—there was hard muscle under the civilised suiting. If she closed her eyes she could remember the exact colours of his tanned skin, the contour of bone and sinew.

And the warmth. If she thought about it she could still feel the tingle where their bare arms had touched. Jemima looked across the busy bar at Niall with his clothes on and her mouth dried.

No flirting? This was much stronger stuff than mere flirting.

She was not at all sure she knew what it was. But she was nearly sure she hadn't done it before. Not when she was a trendy schoolgirl with loads of boyfriends; not as an aspiring model, dating men who couldn't believe their luck; certainly not in the last year.

This feeling was new. Could she handle it?

For a moment she felt paralysed. She did not know what

to do. Go—stay—give an excuse and leave. Face it out…
Jemima put a distracted hand to her temple. For a moment
she nearly turned and fled.

Niall must have seen something of that in her face. He
stood quite still, surveying her. One dark eyebrow rose in a
silent question.

Jemima took hold of herself. This was ridiculous. Of
course she could handle it.

I am never going to be afraid of a man again. Any man.
Only a small voice in her head was saying, *But you're
not afraid of this one. You're afraid of yourself.*

Afraid? *Afraid?* Ridiculous!

Without giving herself time to think about it, Jemima
marched straight up to him and said, all in one breath, 'Hello-
I'll-have-a-white-wine-spritzer-it's-crowded, isn't-it?'

Niall's eyes crinkled with amusement. He waved away
the crowd in the bar as an irrelevance. 'Didn't recognise
me, huh?'

Jemima set her teeth. 'Not just at first, no,' she said with
dignity. 'These Chinese lanterns cast a very peculiar light.'

He was not deceived. 'I told you I cleaned up nice,' he
said complacently.

Two could play at that game. Jemima took a step back
and looked him up and down, the way photographers looked
at a model they were not sure about. She took her time about
it.

'Not bad,' she drawled at last.

She fully expected him to take offence. But instead he
gave a great crack of laughter, as if he were really enjoying
himself.

'You're priceless.' He handed her a glass. 'Your health.'

She was instantly suspicious. 'That doesn't look like a
spritzer.'

'It isn't. It's Pirate's Punch.'

Instantly she was bristling. 'I see. And you know better
than I do what I want to drink?'

Niall looked startled. 'Hey, not me. It's the hotel speci-
ality. Every guest gets one free as the first drink of the
evening. But if you prefer that spritzer—' He crooked a
finger at the barman.

Jemima subsided, feeling a fool.

'No, it's okay. I'll stick with the punch,' she muttered.

But Niall was already giving the order and didn't hear.

'That will be wasted,' said Jemima, at war between irritation and slightly shamefaced good manners.

He shrugged. 'You can switch to that after the punch.'

She shook her head. 'I'm not much of a drinker. One
drink lasts me for ever.'

Those dark eyebrows flew up again. 'How very unusual.'

Irritation won. 'Lots of people don't drink.'

'Not the sort of people who go backpacking alone without
so much as a provisional hotel room to lay their head.'

She laughed angrily. 'Careful, your prejudices are showing. You should get out more.'

And that did wipe the smile off his face.

Pleased, Jemima took a triumphal swig of her punch.

And gasped. Gagged. Then broke down into mighty spluttering.

Niall's expression cleared. He leaned forward solicitously
and thumped her hard between the shoulderblades.

Her eyes watered. But at least she could breathe again.

'Wh-wh-what's in that?' she gasped when she could
speak.

'Fire water, is it?'

He sounded mildly intrigued. Took a sip. Pulled a face.

'Wrong barman on duty tonight.'

He leaned over the bar and hooked up a glass and lots of
ice. There was a big crystal jug of water on the bar and he
filled the glass and gave it to her. Jemima drank about half
straight down in one gulp.

'Thank heavens.'

'Hit the spot, did it? Good. Sorry about the punch. It's
usually full of mango juice. Very refreshing.'

The busy barman came back with Jemima's spritzer. Niall took it from him.

'Do you want me to taste this for you first?'

Jemima laughed weakly, shaking her head. 'I think I'll stick with water for the moment,' she said with feeling.

He put the drink back on the bar. 'I don't blame you.' He was rueful. 'Not one of my better openers.'

In spite of herself, Jemima was charmed. Niall being rueful was very beguiling.

'I'll have to think of a way to make it up to you.'

She waved a magnanimous hand. 'Forget it. I'm breathing again, after all.'

Niall looked down at her. He was smiling, but she detected puzzlement behind his pleasant expression.

She cocked her head. 'What?'

'You know, you're a real contradiction,' he said slowly.

Jemima was taken aback. 'Me?'

'You.'

She scanned his expression, suspecting mockery. But there was none. She shook her head, honestly puzzled. 'Why on earth?'

He seemed to weigh his words. 'I don't want to offend you any more than I have done already.'

Not so beguiling after all, decided Jemima. Her smile froze. She braced herself. 'Oh, why not? Go for it,' she said coldly.

His lips twitched. 'Okay, then. If you really want it. My point is the following: you fire up at the slightest thing, you bristle every time I look at you, and then the barman makes you a toothpaste and vinegar cocktail which nearly chokes you—and you're as sweet as cream about it.'

'Oh.'

To her astonishment, Jemima could feel herself blushing, as if he had paid her a really nice compliment. As if she were shy—and a whole lot more naïve than she could ever remember being, even when she was still a schoolgirl.

As if this were a real date.

She caught herself. This was fantasy land.

She straightened her shoulders. Jemima Dare was cool, cool, *cool*. This laughing stranger didn't know who he was dealing with here. But he would. Oh, boy, he certainly would.

She stared him down. 'I don't think that's much of a contradiction,' she said crisply.

His head went back as if she had suddenly jabbed him in the chest. *Good!*

She shrugged. 'So the barman got his proportions wrong. It's not a hanging offence.'

Niall raised his eyebrows and leaned an elbow on the bar. After his initial surprise he had suddenly become very, very relaxed. Also a lot closer.

'But it's a hanging offence when I look at you?' he drawled.

And of course it was. The way he was looking at her now, anyway. Those heavy-lidded eyes were bright with mockery. But it was not *only* mockery. And they both knew it.

This time she managed not to blush. Though the intent look in his eyes did not make it easy. 'Don't be silly. That's just stupid,' she said hastily.

'You should try standing where I am.'

There was enough truth in that to make her uneasy. Jemima looked away. Her head was ringing with possible answers. *Don't look at me like that. Why are you trying to wind me up? What do you want of me?*

The silence drew out until it hummed like elastic stretched to breaking point. She had to say *something*.

It was not a good thing. 'Well, I guess it's because I don't know you very well.'

'Ah.' It was a note of pure satisfaction.

Jemima winced. Before the words were well out of her mouth she could have kicked herself. It must have sounded like an open invitation to spend the evening together. And he clearly thought the same thing. Or was choosing to take it that way.

Why don't I think before I open my mouth?

Niall smiled at her kindly.

'Okay. Let's start again. I'm Niall Blackthorne,' he said with a charming smile, as if they had just met for the first time. He held out his hand.

Jemima glared. But there was no help for it, not without making exactly the sort of scene she wanted to avoid. Slowly, reluctantly, as if it was being dragged away from her body, she put her own hand into his.

'H-hello,' she managed. She didn't know whom she was more furious with—Niall Blackthorne for playing games with her, or herself for not handling it better.

His palm was cool and strong. Her fingers tingled when they touched his. Jemima swallowed and tried to ignore the slight ringing in her ears.

Niall shook her hand with brisk formality and let her have her hand back.

'I'm at Pirate's Point until the weekend. How long are you here for, Ms Cooper? Or may I call you Jay Jay?'

Jemima shivered and clamped both hands round her glass of water.

That phony name was going to be a mistake. In that caressing voice it felt horribly intimate. In the business everyone called her Jemima. Only her sister called her Jay Jay. Hearing Niall Blackthorne use the name felt like handing him a key and an open invitation to stroll into her life. And she had a nasty suspicion that he knew it.

Why don't I think?

She bit her lip. 'Call me whatever you like,' she said curtly. 'I'm leaving tomorrow.'

He gave her a long, slow smile.

It seemed she could feel it, right through to where the blood beat at the base of her throat. It felt as if it was suffocating her. Jemima put up a hand to quiet it…

And he saw. His smile widened.

'Then we only have tonight,' he said blandly. 'I take that as a challenge.'

Jemima's eyes flared. 'What do you mean, a challenge?'

'Not to waste a moment of it,' he told her with another of those slow, meaningful smiles that scrambled her brains. 'Let's go.'

'G-go?'

But he was holding out a commanding hand. And, to Jemima's inner fury, she went with him. Meek as a rounded-up sheep, she thought, disgusted at herself. But she still went.

He took her through the gate and out onto the beach. Before them the sea murmured and lapped.

'Ah. That sort of challenge,' said Jemima, detaching her hand and sounding brightly self-possessed. 'Romantic walk along the beach. Original!'

'Cynic.' His voice was full of laughter. 'Look at those stars.'

'Think I'll concentrate on keeping upright just for the moment, thank you.'

Her espadrilles were divinely comfortable and easy to pack, but they slithered all over the place on the powdery sand.

'Hang on to me,' said Niall.

If there had been the slightest hint of triumph in his voice Jemima would have told him what she thought of his teasing and stalked away. But there was not. He sounded neutral, innocent and mildly helpful. Damn him.

'Very kind.' She did not mean it.

Niall Blackthorne took her hand and put it firmly into the crook of his arm. 'Take small steps. You're trying to stride out too much. That's when you skid.'

His touch set her unruly pulses galloping again.

What is wrong with me? I regularly get wrapped up in the arms of the most beautiful men in the business. They don't do this to me!

'Thank you,' she said in a strangled voice.

The breeze off the sea was cool. She refused to shiver, but they were walking so close that he picked it up.

'Cold?'

'Maybe a little.'

He stopped at once and took off his jacket. Before Jemima could think of a thing to say he had swung it round her shoulders and taken her hand again, urging them on.

'Better?'

The jacket was surprisingly heavy. The silky lining slithered along her exposed skin like a live creature. She felt embraced by it. Soothed and somehow protected. And so warm! It was like cuddling up in front of a warm fire on a cold night. Like basking in sunshine.

Like being loved.

Oh, boy, am I in trouble here.

'Very toasty,' Jemima said brightly, and much, much too loudly. She did not look at him.

She held the jacket clutched round her as carefully as if it were a king's cloak. And when they went up the steps to the terrace restaurant she surrendered it reluctantly. But there really was no reason to hang onto it once they were out of the faint sea breeze. She let it go as Al seated her.

'Nice quiet table,' said Al.

He exchanged another of those complicated masculine looks with Niall. She wasn't supposed to notice them, thought Jemima. But instantly she was on her guard.

She shook her head at another rum punch, accepted mango juice and said casually when he left, 'You must have known each other a long time.'

Niall was shrugging himself back into his jacket. He looked up at that, surprised.

'Al and me? That's shrewd of you.'

She had the impression he did not like her being shrewd. She said excusingly, 'You seem—comfortable with each other.'

'Well, we've bumped into each other in various resorts

round the world. Must be fifteen years since we first met. Maybe more.'

'Friends, then?' she concluded.

He looked into the little candle that burned in the middle of their table, his expression oddly sober. 'Maybe. Nearly.'

Jemima was intrigued. 'Nearly friends? What does that mean?'

Niall shrugged. 'We go back a long time. We've seen a lot together. I guess that makes us friends of a sort, yes.'

'Tell.'

He looked up suddenly. Jemima was startled. How could she have thought he was not good-looking? In the candle-light he was real heartbreaker material.

'You want the story of my criminal past?' he mocked. But it was gentle mockery this time. 'Okay, then. You asked for it.'

He was very, very funny. There was one tale of a card sharp in Macao when Al had been a greenhorn of nineteen. Niall, scarcely older, had already known how to suss out the villains. But not before the two boys had ended up lurking at the train depot and getting soaked in mud during a sleepless night.

Jemima laughed until she had a stitch. She put a hand to her side, chuckling.

Niall was hurt. 'Women are hard,' he complained.

And launched into another story, this time of a woman with a gun and a grievance on another island paradise.

'Nearly ended Al's career,' he said with relish.

'What happened?' said Jemima, weak with laughter.

'Niall talked her out of it,' said Al, appearing at her elbow with mango juice and Niall's beer. 'He's good at that.' He produced a handwritten menu card with a flourish. 'Ellie says have the red snapper.'

Jemima glanced quickly at the card and was taken aback. 'I can't eat all this,' she said, from the heart.

There was butternut squash soup, a salad of rocket with grapefruit and passionfruit seed dressing, pan-fried red snapper with local vegetables, cheeses, a vacherin with banana, rum and walnuts.

Al looked hurt. 'It's all good fresh food.'

'But I can't remember when I last had cheese. Let alone a dessert.'

Niall laughed. 'Take it a step at a time. You'll be surprised how easy it is.'

Jemima looked up sharply. She was not at all sure that he was talking about the food.

She shook the menu card. 'Just to read this makes my mouth water. And my eyes bulge.' She sighed ruefully. 'Followed by waistline, if I'm not careful.'

Niall gave her another of his most charming smiles. Jemima's suspicion redoubled.

'Give it a chance,' he said. 'Like walking on the beach. Small steps, one at a time. You'll get there.'

Her eyebrows twitched together savagely. Not suspicious any more. Certain. He was laughing at her *and* he was trying to seduce her. What sort of an idiot did he think she was?

This time the smile was downright caressing. 'We'll take everything. And see how far the lady wants to go,' Niall told Al wickedly.

Jemima met his eyes and said deliberately, 'The lady knows exactly how far she is going to go.' Then, to Al, 'Just the fish and the salad, please.'

Al was philosophical. 'Shame. Maybe another time.' He made a note. 'Are you going to the casino tonight?'

Niall was serene. 'Of course.'

Al shifted from foot to foot. 'Sure? I mean—a night off wouldn't hurt.'

Niall cocked his head. 'Listening to gossip, Al?'

Al looked uncomfortable. 'You know your own business best,' he said unconvincingly. 'I'll tell Ellie two fish, then, shall I?' And he almost took off at a run.

Jemima watched his disorderly retreat with astonishment. 'What was that about?'

'Al trying to save me from myself.' Niall picked up his beer and toasted her silently.

'What?'

'He was suggesting I spend a charming evening with you instead of going over to the Casino Caraibe as I usually do,' he interpreted.

'Oh.'

Jemima digested this. She was not pleased.

Why did Niall have to have it suggested to him? Not that she would go, of course. Of course she wouldn't. But still, he should have thought of it for himself. Men did not normally need prompting to ask her on a date.

She narrowed her eyes at him. 'Thank you, Al, 'she muttered.

Niall looked startled.

So startled that Jemima was even more annoyed. 'Well?' she said pugnaciously. 'Are you going to ask me to go to the casino with you, then?'

'No,' said Niall with unflattering promptness.

Jemima gasped.

He seemed to work out that he was not giving satisfaction. He said, on a faint note of apology, 'I'm a professional gambler. It's my work. Would you take a complete stranger into the office with you?'

Jemima was so flabbergasted that all she could think of to say was, 'I don't work in an office.'

He shrugged. 'Wherever. My point is that you don't party when you're earning the monthly wage.' He gave her one of his slow, seductive smiles. 'Ask me any other time but the evening and I'll be head of the queue.'

Jemima was outraged. For a moment she could hardly speak. 'You just overwhelm me.'

He grinned suddenly. When he smiled like that, his eyes crinkled up at the corners and two deep clefts appeared on either side of that sensual mouth. They were just begging to be touched. Stroked.

Jemima sat on her hands. Fast.

'Overwhelm you? I don't think any guy would over-whelm you.' he said ruefully. 'Certainly not me. I just annoy you. Even when I'm not trying to.'

That shook her. 'You've been *trying* to annoy me?'

His eyes danced. 'You're beautiful when you're angry, Miss Cooper.'

At last Jemima's sense of humour reasserted itself. Two could play at this game. 'I'm beautiful all the time,' she said calmly. 'Got the references to prove it.'

She watched with glee as his eyebrows hit his hairline.

He recovered well. 'Poets write you sonnets?'

Jemima put her head on one side. She was enjoying her-self. 'Something like that.'

Niall was clearly intrigued. 'You're an artist's model? An artist's inspiration? A weather girl?'

She shook her head, laughing. 'Keep trying.'

Niall snapped his fingers. 'You are Kuan Yin, the goddess of good fortune. Come down to earth in human form.'

'Goddess is good,' she said naughtily.

He did the crinkled eyes trick again. 'Then I'm changing my mind,' he announced. 'If you're the goddess of good fortune, then Al was right. You're coming with me to the casino.'

Jemima stopped laughing abruptly. 'What?'

He raised his glass to her. 'Welcome to the world of Niall Blackthorne, adventurer.'

CHAPTER FOUR

THERE was a covered walkway to the casino. It was lit by
Chinese lanterns and discreet low-level lights tucked among
the bushes. It was pretty and safe and civilised, like a path
through a suburban garden.

But as they walked Jemima heard things rustling in the
dark beyond the lights, things that darted and croaked and
grunted. Beyond the lights, it did not sound safe and civilised at all. And the man beside her was no reassurance. He
was much too unpredictable.

Niall Blackthorne, adventurer! What did that mean?

She said dryly, 'If the rhinoceros stampedes, can I count
on you to save me?'

He looked down at her and did that sexy eyebrow-flick
again. 'Rhinoceros?'

She waved a hand at the shadows of bushes beyond the
walkway. 'The one that's stamping around in the undergrowth.'

Niall gave a shout of laughter. 'Sounds as if you haven't
taken Africa in yet.'

Jemima bridled. 'What do you mean?'

'A rhinoceros would be in full surround-sound.'

'You've met lots of them, I suppose?'

He shook his head, still laughing. 'You don't meet a rhinoceros. You get out of its way fast. I've legged it away
from a couple, yes.'

Jemima's eyes narrowed to slits. 'So that's what an adventurer is,' she mused.

That threw him. 'I'm sorry?'

'I was wondering what an adventurer was, exactly. And

now you've answered the problem for me.' She beamed at him, all innocence. 'Someone who runs away from wildlife.'

But Niall was not crushed by the put-down, not a smidgeon. He said with odious kindness, 'You know, you really have got to visit Africa. You've got a lot to learn about nature. Let me tell you, there's wildlife and wildlife.'

Jemima did not like being patronised. She said sharply, 'And I suppose you're personally acquainted with whatever it is that's clog-dancing in the bushes over there?'

His eyes danced. 'Well, at a guess I'd say it's an agouti.'

Jemima had never heard the word before. 'You made that up.'

He shook his head solemnly. 'Cross my heart.'

'I don't believe you. Nothing could be called an agouti,' Jemima said positively. 'It sounds halfway between a zombie and an angora rabbit.'

'Actually, it's a sort of grown-up guinea pig.'

'Oh, pu-lease.'

'Why does the woman not believe me?' he asked a Chinese lantern, mock mournful.

Jemima was crushing. 'Because I had guinea pigs as a child. I know they only come in one size.'

He shook his head. 'You sure you've been to the Caribbean before? They're not hard to spot.'

'The last time I was in the Caribbean I—' Too late she realised where this was taking her and skidded to a halt.

'Yes?' he asked mildly. 'The last time you—?'

'Wasn't looking for guinea pigs,' she finished lamely.

She bit her lip. What a terrible liar she was turning out to be! She might just as well given him her name and profession from the start. Along with her agent's phone number!

'So what were you looking for?' He sounded amused. But wary too.

'What are you?' she said disagreeably. 'The Spanish Inquisition?'

'Just trying to get my facts clear. I mean, I thought you

said that you were a great traveller. But your experience seems a bit limited.'

Jemima stopped dead and rounded on him, hands on hips. She said between her teeth, 'My experience is not limited at all.'

He didn't say anything. Instead he stopped too, and looked her calmly up and down. And then that wicked eyebrow went up again.

Jemima could have danced with rage. The only thing that stopped her was the thought that that was exactly what he was trying to goad her into.

She stepped away from him and started to walk again. Or march.

'Well, I've certainly never gambled for a living.' It was poisonously sweet. 'Come and show me what that bit of adventuring is like.'

She set a heck of a pace to the casino. But Niall never broke out of a stroll. He just lengthened his stride and kept up with her easily. It was as irritating as everything else about him, Jemima decided.

She steamed into the plush interior with a face like thunder.

It was like a futuristic hotel. Bigger than it looked from the outside, it was built in an octagon. Great walls of windows gave onto the sea on six sides. Small cocktail tables were set all round the outer walls, where people could sit and play two-hander games or sip their drinks and watch the stars. But the middle of the room was where it all happened.

'It's like a skating rink,' said Jemima, fascinated.

There were card tables and roulette tables and games of backgammon. There were brilliant banks of lights over the tables. There was muted conversation. But mostly the sound was the click of chips, the whirr of the spinning wheel, the slap of cards coming out of the shoe. And the chink of ice and the click of ultra-high heels on a floor as dark and shining as the sky outside.

'It's like a party,' she said, wondering. She gave a crack of sudden laughter. 'And I'm underdressed. Well, that's a first. A *very* classy party.'

Niall was at her shoulder. He looked down at her at that. 'Is it? Look again.'

Waiters wove expertly through the crowd, lifting their trays of drinks high above the heads of the crowd. But, for all the diamonds and four-star tans, there were no party buzz. No laughter. No music. Instead the air was tense with attention.

'I see what you mean,' she said slowly. 'Everyone is either playing or watching someone else.'

'Your first time in a casino too, huh?'

Her first instinct was to deny it. She did not like this man writing her off as inexperienced. Then common sense reasserted itself.

'Yes,' she said ruefully. 'Never got closer than a James Bond movie.'

'I thought not.'

In spite of that common sense she stiffened. 'Does it show?' she said with an attempt at lightness.

'Yes.'

She lifted her chin, all lightness dissolving. 'Are you calling me naïve?'

'Wouldn't dare,' he said promptly.

She didn't believe him.

'How naïve do you think I am?' There was an edge to her voice.

'Haven't a clue,' said Niall, with a ghost of smile. 'I'll look into it.'

And what did that mean? The words could have been a veiled threat. But Jemima had been on the receiving end of threats from Basil Blane for months now, and it didn't feel like a threat. It felt—if that weren't totally stupid—like a promise. She gave a little shiver of anticipation.

'Only not just now. I've got to go to work. So stick with me, look charming, and don't talk.'

He bought her the orange juice she asked for. He paid in dollars and the price made her eyes widen. Jemima had drunk orange juice in the most exclusive clubs in London, Paris and New York and this place beat them all.

'Wow. This is not for the guy on a budget, is it?' She remembered the scruffy beach bum gear in which he'd first met her and conscience smote her. Professional gambler or not, he did not look as if he could afford this. 'You must let me pay—'

He shook his head. 'Business expense. But thank you.'

He gave her a sudden smile. The sweetness of it made her blink. So did the way her heart seemed to go into overdrive.

Oh, no. That's all I need.

It was that, more than his instructions, that kept her quiet as a mouse as they strolled round the casino floor.

He watched each table with interest for a while, before taking her on with a word and a smile. After a while Jemima realised that he had a strategy. She was dying to ask him if he had a system. But you didn't interrupt a man when he was working!

Eventually he stopped at the blackjack table. He slid his arm casually round her waist and she held her breath. His body was so lithe, so warm under the tuxedo. And the arm was almost possessive. Nobody had stood beside her in public with a possessive arm round her since...

She thought about it. Well, ever. Basil had not put his arm round her. And with Basil hovering jealously no one else had either. And since Basil she had not let anyone get close enough.

A new experience, then. Jemima shivered voluptuously and lost track of time.

So she did not know how long he watched the game. She almost jumped when one of the gamblers got up from the table and Niall removed his arm.

'I'll sit in for a while.'

The dealer, sober in a tuxedo nearly as elegant as Niall's own, nodded.

Niall slid into the vacated seat and the dealer started to deal again.

Jemima found there was a lump in her throat. Help, what was wrong with her? A man she did not know took his arm away from her waist and she felt bereft? *Get a life, Jemima.*

Without taking his eye off the green baize and the other players, Niall reached up and took her hand. He put it on his shoulder. 'Bring me luck, sweetness.'

It was like an unexpected present. A perfect moment. A thrill and a coming home.

It was like being loved.

Jemima stood like a statue. Her thoughts whirled.

Like being loved? How pathetic is that?

But it felt so right. And that was a new experience too.

It was some minutes before she brought her attention back to what was happening on the tables. Niall appeared to be losing. But he did not seem to mind. His voice stayed amused, his smile rueful, his stance casual. Only, under her fingers, his shoulder was taut as a tiger about to spring.

And then it seemed his luck changed. A little. Then more. Then he put down a big sum on the last turn of the cards and it came up. The players and the dealer stayed impassive, but there was an almost visible frisson among the watchers.

He put up his hand to cover hers.

'Bored, darling? Just one more. Then we'll go and look at the stars.'

It sounded perfect, the indulgent lover placating a bored beauty. But for all the caressing note in his voice he did not look at her, not for a moment. He did not take his eyes off the dealer.

He won again. Their table was beginning to attract a crowd. He pushed back his chair.

'I'm out.' He stood up and nodded to the dealer and his fellow players. 'Good game. Thank you. Now, darling, let's go find some moonlight.'

He turned to Jemima and that warm, wonderful arm came round her again. But this time her heart did not miss a beat.

I'm just window dressing. An alibi for a professional gambler. How clever he is.

It was chilling.

He walked close. Jemima thought she felt his cheek brush against her hair. She swallowed and stared straight ahead, dry-eyed.

Then she heard in her ear, 'Keep walking and look devoted. Manager at ten o'clock.'

At that she did look up at him. He did a very good devoted lover, she found. Her heart felt squeezed like a lemon.

A tall, authoritative man appeared at Niall's elbow. 'Mr Blackthorne? Leaving early this evening?'

Niall said easily, 'Ah, but tonight I have company, Henry.'

The manager paced beside them. 'We'll see you again, I hope?'

Niall nodded. 'You can count on it.'

He cashed their chips. Jemima was startled to see the amount of money on the draft.

'Wow,' she said, momentarily diverted from her strangely hurting heart.

'Quit while you're ahead,' he said lightly. He grinned at the manager. 'Don't worry, Henry. I'll be back tomorrow.'

The manager smiled. 'You know you're always welcome.' He held the door open for them. 'See you soon, I hope. Goodnight, Mr Blackthorne. Goodnight, *madame*.'

Jemima's eyebrows flew up.

'Cor,' she said, as they started back under the Chinese lanterns. 'Haven't been called *madame* before.'

'You've led a sheltered life.'

She shook her head vigorously. 'Don't think it's that at all. I think it's because I've never walked out with a guy shipping a quarter of a million dollars in his inside pocket.'

'Henry won't be worried about that.' Niall's voice was cynical. 'He was a lot more worried last week.'

Jemima was intrigued. It was a relief. Better than thinking about that unexpected little pain around her heart, anyway.

'What happened last week?'

'I hit a losing streak.'

She was puzzled. 'But isn't that good for the casino?'

'Not if they think you can't honour your debts.'

'Oh.'

'You don't ask professional gamblers if they're on a losing streak,' Niall said in an academic tone. 'But Henry got very confiding, for a couple of nights. There must have been rumours in Queen's Town.'

'Maybe it's because you looked as if you were odd-jobbing for the hotel,' suggested Jemima tartly. 'Kind of the jet-set equivalent of doing the washing up when you can't pay the restaurant bill.'

Niall gave another one of his great shouts of laughter. 'I didn't think of that.'

She slid a look at him from under her lashes. He looked ultra-relaxed: smooth, sophisticated, in control. It was impossible to imagine him being worried about anything.

'Were you worried at all?' she ventured.

'Counting up my losses, you mean?' He sounded astonished. 'No. Losing is against my principles.'

'You and the casino, both,' said Jemima dryly.

'That's why Henry and I understand each other. We both take the long view.'

Enlightenment dawned. 'So *that's* why you're going back tomorrow. So they get some of it back!'

There was a small silence.

'Shrewd,' he said at last. She had the feeling he wasn't very pleased about it.

'So I'm right?'

'Oh, yes. The professional never takes too much. It gets you banned.'

'Banned?' She was startled. 'Do you cheat?'

'You don't have to cheat,' he said dryly. 'Just be cleverer than the house.'

They walked in silence for a moment.

To anyone watching they must look like the last word in glamorous success. The tall, handsome man in his impeccable tuxedo. The leggy redhead, not so formally dressed but making up for that in sheer beauty. Anyone watching would think: the perfect couple.

Only they were not a couple. They were walking just that hand's breadth apart. But it could have been the Bering Straits between them.

In this heavily romantic setting Izzy and her Dominic would have had their arms round each other, stopping every so often to kiss and laugh. Pepper and Steven would have walked hand in hand, Pepper's head drooping onto his shoulder to look at the moon.

Jemima felt that inexplicable pinching round her heart again. She moved even further away from Niall and gave him a bright, social smile.

'So, do you have a system?' she said in a brittle voice. It was what Izzy called her How Nice To Meet You, Mr Mayor voice. It went with Jemima Dare, international celebrity, professional to her fingertips. It was the voice—and the technique—she used when she launched ships and opened nightclubs. Keep them talking about themselves and they thought that you were wonderful.

Niall showed no signs of thinking she was wonderful. He looked at her frowning. 'What's wrong?'

'Nothing.' If possible her smile got even wider. 'I thought you needed a system to beat the casinos at their own game.'

His look was searching. 'What did I say?'

Jemima's unheld hand felt like ice. She clutched her arms round herself and upped the smile wattage. 'Nothing.' Her brightness was almost feverish by now. 'Isn't it true, then?'

He shrugged, letting the subject go. At least for the moment.

'It doesn't work like that. There's no system that will beat a roulette wheel. They all have zeroes. In the States, lots of casinos have double zeroes. That doubles the house advantage. You can lose a lot of money thinking you have a system at roulette.' He paused. 'What *is* it, Jay Jay?'

If only he hadn't sounded so gentle all of a sudden! If only he hadn't used the name she had given him, the name that only people who loved her ever used! It nearly undid her.

She blinked rapidly, so there was not a hint of tears in her eyes, and pretended she hadn't heard.

'So, how does a professional gambler make a living?' she asked, still in Nightclub Opening mode.

'What?'

Still gentle. Disarmingly, treacherously gentle. And was he watching her eyelashes?

Jemima turned her head away. She could flirt with the best of them, but somehow, just now, she really, really didn't want to. Not tonight, among the Chinese lanterns, with whispering undergrowth on either side of the path and the sea lulling and hushing in the distance.

She repeated the question, not looking at him.

Niall seemed to pull himself together. 'Well, the best way is at cards. If you have a good memory, and the right sort of mindset, you can count the cards that have gone. Which means that as the game goes on the odds shorten considerably against what might come up. Blackjack is the best.'

'Don't the casinos mind?'

'Sure. If they catch you doing it, they ban you.'

'Ban you?' She was startled into looking at him. 'It's against the law?'

'No. Counting cards is legal. But not many people can do it. So when someone wins too regularly, the casino security staff watch. If you're cheating they prosecute. If you're counting cards, they ease you out. There's even a blacklist. And I'm not on it, because I take care to lose enough.' He gave her a smile, devastating in its sweetness. 'Now, can we talk about you, please?'

'No,' she said on pure reflex.

He nodded slowly. 'I—see. Well, what about a walk

along the beach, then? Seems a shame to waste all this moonlight.'

Jemima's heart leaped. She caught it back hard, like someone grabbing at a runaway kite at the last moment.

'Let's waste it,' she said firmly. 'I'm tired.' She gave a theatrical yawn to prove it.

He did respond for a moment.

Then, 'Liar,' he said softly.

'I *am*.'

'You spent the whole afternoon snoozing. That will deal with it.' He paused. 'Unless you're older than you look, of course.'

Jemima recognised deliberate provocation. She glared. 'I am jet-lagged,' she announced pugnaciously. 'On my time it's six o'clock in the morning.'

'Nearly time for breakfast, then.'

She gave a sudden snort of laughter. 'Not in my world.'

His eyes narrowed. 'Yes, we must talk about that some time.'

'About what?'

'Your world.'

She stopped laughing. 'What about it?' she said uneasily.

'It interests me.' He gave her a long, lustful look and lowered his voice to the soles of his feet. 'You interest me.'

Jemima might have trouble with her heart and her blood pressure around Niall Blackthorne, but sexy looks were nine-to-five routine to her. Every male model she had ever worked out with practised that husky throb in the voice for when he got his break in the movies.

She gave Niall a long, lustful—and rather better—look right back, and said, 'You lie in your teeth.'

He blinked, genuinely taken aback for a moment. Then his lips twitched. 'So that makes two of us. You're not jet-lagged. You're firing on all cylinders.'

Jemima ground her teeth. She had walked right into that one!

He put out hand. 'Come on. You're woman enough for a walk in the moonlight. Aren't you?'

Well, put like that, of course, there was not much she could do about it. Not and keep her dignity—to say nothing of her self-respect.

She didn't let him hold her hand, though. That would have been too much to ask.

CHAPTER FIVE

IT DIDN'T take long to leave the lanterns behind. Soon the casino was no more than a glimmer of lights on the horizon. And then they rounded an outcrop, and even that was gone.

At once all the noises of the night seemed to come closer. The metallic rustle of the breeze in the palm trees. The gurgle of a stream falling down the hillside to their right somewhere close. The pulse-beat of the sea, like a patient animal, to their left. Jemima swallowed.

'All very elemental,' she said brightly.

Or tried to. The breeze tossed her words up and threaded them like paper. It was as if she had no substance at all. At least, not compared with all the breathing, murmuring life out there in the darkness. She didn't want Niall to hold her hand, but even so... She stepped closer to him and stayed there.

He looked down at her. 'Cold?'

She shook her head. 'No. Just a bit—well, outclassed, maybe.'

'Outclassed?'

She gestured towards the sea. She could not see it. But she could see a path of moonlight, shifting and rippling across the unseen waves.

'Look at that. It's like being on the edge of another world. You see why people believed in all that stuff—mermaids and kingdoms under the sea and magic. I've never seen anything like it before. So beautiful. But a bit frightening.'

'I was brought up by the sea.'

'Don't tell me,' said Jemima, resigned. 'You can take all this in your stride.'

There was a laugh in his voice. 'Well, it doesn't frighten me.'

She said, in a moment of pure instinct, 'But then nothing frightens you.'

'*What?*' He stopped dead.

Jemima stopped too, and turned to face him.

It must be down to the night. Or the heaving, whispering sea. Or that tantalising moonlight way behind his shoulder. Something magical had happened. Suddenly Jemima was telling the truth without reservation or restraint. She had no idea how she knew it was the truth. She just *did*.

'You can handle anything, can't you?' she said slowly. 'You don't care about anything, so you can deal with it all.'

There was a slight, tense pause.

Then, 'Where did that come from?' He did not sound pleased.

They were so close she had to tip her head back to look at him. 'Are you saying it isn't true?'

He said slowly, 'That sounds like an accusation.'

It did too. She had no idea why. 'It's not human not to care about anything,' she said grumpily.

'You'd rather I got in a panic when the unexpected happens? A panicker would have left you at the airport to fend for yourself,' he pointed out. His tone was mocking. But underneath there was something like real anger.

Jemima did not stop to think about that. 'Panic?' she scoffed. 'What was there to panic about?'

His hands shot out. He took hold of her shoulders and held her still in front of him, as if she had been about to strike him. Or run.

Did his women usually run? she thought ironically. And then it caught up with her—his women? *His* women?

What was she thinking of? She wasn't one of his women! Never in a million years.

But she still stayed there, letting him hold her.

He said, 'You don't know, do you? You just—don't—know.'

'Know what?' Suddenly she was breathless.

For a moment he did not answer. Instead, he scanned her face as if it would tell him all her secrets. What on earth did he think he could see in the moonlight?

Except—Jemima realised with a little shock that she was seeing a different Niall Blackthorne in the moonlight. In spite of the shadows—maybe because of the shadows—he was suddenly a stranger. Not the arrogant beach bum. Not the suave gambler either. He looked taller, graver. There were wasp stings of moonlight along those haughty cheekbones. And suddenly she thought—You're not haughty; you're *alone*.

And diabolically handsome in the moonlight.

Something inside Jemima woke up and started to thrum. It was like a butterfly starting to pile-drive its way out of the chrysalis. It seemed to shake her whole body, scarcely perceptible but somehow irresistible.

It was exciting. It was utterly new. It was terrifying.

She put a hand to her midriff, to still her too rapid breaths. Niall did not notice.

He said slowly, 'Who are you? Who are you, really?'

Jemima blinked. 'What?'

She must have sounded stupid, she realised, but she couldn't believe it. Couldn't he sense this pile-driver that was shaking her to her foundations? Didn't he feel it too?

Niall shook his head. The dark hair gleamed in the moonlight. His eyes were fathomless.

'Well, your own story is a lie. You're no traveller. And my hypothesis looks as if it's wrong too. You've never been inside a casino in your life, have you?'

'Your hypothesis?' Jemima echoed. Suddenly she felt very cold.

'That you are here to investigate me,' said Niall, with complete sang froid. 'You wouldn't be the first.'

'Oh.'

Jemima hugged her arms round her. The breeze off the sea seemed to have got a lot colder.

'Not that you were very good at it. Miss Jay Jay Cooper, travelling under the name of Dare.' His voice was ironic.

She stepped out of his hold. That damned credit card!

'Isn't it illegal to hack into a hotel's records?' she asked distantly.

'Who needs to hack? I looked at your register card.'

She bit her lip. 'That's sneaky.'

He was unrepentant. 'But practical.'

'Like asking me to have dinner with you,' Jemima said on a note of discovery.

'That was in the nature of damage limitation. If you were investigating me I wanted to keep you under my eye.' His voice was hard. 'What better way than to wander off hand in hand to the casino?'

Jemima put both hands behind her back. 'Sneaky and nasty.'

He shrugged. 'Gets results.'

'Does it?'

She looked up at the diamond chip stars behind his shoulders. If she kept her eyes wide, looking at the sky, they weren't going to fill up with silly tears. There would have been stars like this over the Gardens of the Hesperides. Paradise would have had nights like this. Only in Paradise people didn't spy and lie and play games.

'Does it really get results?' asked Jemima bleakly.

'Oh, yes.'

'So what has it got you tonight?' she challenged him.

'Well, I know you have two names.' He paused. 'At least two names. That's a clue.'

'Clue to what?'

'That you're not all you seem.'

She was oddly hurt. 'Who is?' she said, her voice as hard as his.

He noticed that. 'You mind?'

'Mind you snooping in my records?' Jemima was incredulous. 'Of course I mind.'

'Not that. You mind me finding out.'

A chill touched her. 'You've found out nothing,' she spat. *'Nothing.'*

'You think so?' But it wasn't a challenge.

She stared at him, the sudden anger dying as quickly as it had flamed up. 'What?' she said, uncertainly.

'I've found out lots.'

'Oh, yeah? Like what.'

'Like—you guard yourself as if you've got someone on your trail too. Like—you don't hold hands lightly.' His voice softened. 'Like—when you laugh, your whole face changes.

As if he could not stop himself, he touched her lower lip. It was a fleeting brush of the fingers, light as a cobweb. And it was gone almost before she had time to register it. But it set her blood pounding through her veins.

She could not help herself. She swallowed.

He said almost inaudibly, 'Like—I want to know you properly.'

She stared at him, silenced.

He looked back, his eyes grave in the silvery shadows. He had no right to look so—so *serious*, Jemima thought. So concerned. He was a beach bum who lived by outwitting casinos. He had set trap after trap for her tonight. Heaven knows how many of them she had fallen into! She was out of her mind if she thought she could rely on him, even for a moment. Even for a starlit night in Paradise.

He said, 'Don't leave tomorrow. Stay at Pirate's Point. Give us a chance.'

She said nothing.

It could have been another trap. Jemima, listening to her blood, knew very well that it might be. And knew that she would risk it. Had to risk it.

'I'll think about it,' she said.

But she knew she would stay.

The next morning she picked up some fruit from the breakfast table and wandered down onto the beach. There were several people already there sunbathing. But nobody took any notice of her, she saw, pleased.

She finished her pineapple and looked longingly at the sea. But she still had to buy a swimsuit. So she contented herself with swirling her hands about in the salt water before wandering out to the reception desk.

Al was there. He looked up, smiling. 'Hi? Sleep well?'

'A log would have had a hard time keeping up,' she said gravely. 'Any messages for me?'

'No.'

Jemima drew a long sigh of satisfaction. *I've won this one, then, Basil.* She felt as if she had taken off a particularly vicious boned basque. You didn't notice as long as you were wearing it. But when you took it off—bliss. She gave him a great big smile.

He blinked. 'Want to let the folks know you're safe?'

'Oh. No. Well, I hadn't thought about it. Maybe.' She put her head on one side. She had a gap in her diary, sure, but that didn't mean the agency would be happy to lose sight of her. To say nothing of Izzy and Pepper. 'Yeah,' she decided. 'You're probably right. I really ought to let the family know where I am. Is there an internet café anywhere in town?'

He grinned. 'If you want to access your e-mail, you can use the computer in the office. I give you a card and it goes on your bill.'

'Great.' She looked round the lobby. 'I don't suppose you have a boutique too? I meant to pick up a swimsuit at the airport. But the shops in London were closed and in Barbados they hadn't opened. And here—' She shook her head sadly.

Al handed over a key card and waved a hand in the direction of a discreet door behind a palm tree. 'No boutique, sorry. You really will have to go into town for that. I heard Niall say at breakfast that he was going to take you. Just as well.'

She was studying the card but her head reared up at that. 'What?'

Al let out a crack of laughter. 'Didn't he tell you, then?' He shook his head tolerantly. 'Boy, that man gets away with murder.' He was clearly torn between admiration and a sense that it wasn't fair.

Jemima wasn't torn at all. She stiffened. 'Oh?'

Al shook his head, oblivious. 'He's such a charmer!' he said wistfully. 'It's always the same.'

'Really?' Jemima was frosty.

'Every time he comes to stay. Cuts a swathe through the female guests. Why, only this week—' He broke off. 'And here he is.'

It sounded as if he was congratulating her on Niall bothering to put in an appearance at all, thought Jemima, fuming.

'So he is,' she said, deceptively affable.

'Gorgeous morning.' Niall was clearly in tearing spirits. 'Ready to go?'

This morning he was wearing Bermuda shorts that showed off more muscular mahogany brown leg than Jemima wanted to think about.

His chest was bare too. Hair-roughened. And brown as a nut. She averted her eyes.

'I may have got the wrong end of the stick,' she told the potted palm tree with dignity. 'I didn't sign up to go on a date.'

Niall was not noticeably cast down. 'You said you'd spend the day with me. Can't back out now.'

'Oh, yes, I can,' she flashed, before she could stop herself. At once she drew a deep steadying breath. Dignity, she reminded herself. Dignity, Jemima! This man needs putting in his place. You won't do it by playground spitting. 'I mean, it's not convenient.'

His eyebrows rose. 'How come?'

That threw her. 'What?'

'How can it suddenly be not convenient? You're not doing anything else. Yesterday you were talking of flying out today. That's an empty diary.'

Jemima's hand clenched so hard that the corners of the little key card dug into her palm. Inspired, she said, 'I need to talk to people. Send a few e-mails. I don't know how long it will take.'

His eyebrows rose. But he didn't say anything.

'Sorry,' she added unconvincingly.

He was not buying it. And he was not playing nice either. 'Lost your bottle?' he said softly.

Flustered, Jemima looked at Al. The man was agog, not even trying to hide his avid interest. And Niall didn't seem to care—or even notice. She could have screamed.

Dignity, she reminded herself feverishly.

She gave a laugh which didn't sound too bad in the circumstances and said lightly, 'That's silly.'

'Is it?'

This was a provocation too far. Jemima's eyes narrowed to slits. 'Look, sunshine, when I agreed to see you today I thought we were both staying at Pirate's Point,' she said crisply. 'I wasn't expecting a Magical Mystery Tour.'

'So adjust your expectations,' Niall advised.

Behind the desk, Al gave a choke of laughter. Jemima glared at him and he converted it rapidly into a cough. She decided that a little revenge was in order.

'You mean, let you get away with murder?' she cooed.

Niall frowned. 'I'm sorry?'

Al suddenly looked alarmed. Jemima beamed at him.

'That's what Al was telling me is *your* usual expectation,' she explained, at her sweetest. 'Maybe you're the one who needs to adjust?'

Both men were utterly silenced.

Definitely a round to me, she thought with satisfaction. She floated off without a backward look. But behind her she heard Niall say, 'Gee, thanks, buddy.' Unseen, she grinned from ear to ear.

The door behind the palm tree proved to lead into a small

but efficient business centre. There was a computer, a fax machine, a printer, a shelf of international directories and four clocks on the wall, showing the time round the world.

She consulted the computer handbook, enabled it rapidly, and then sat down to access her e-mail messages.

The agency was panicking. Where was she? Why hadn't she called? She hadn't forgotten her meeting at the Dorchester next Wednesday, had she? That was easy. 'No,' she typed, and sent it at once. Then conscience struck and she sent them a second e-mail with the hotel's contact details. 'But only if you absolutely have to get in touch,' she added warningly. 'I'm chilling out big time here.'

Pepper wanted to know if Jemima would mind wearing a bridesmaid's dress in rose-pink. That was easy too. 'Yes!!!' she sent. 'Put me in pink and I resign *now*.'

And Izzy—well, Izzy was wildly happy, more in love than she had ever imagined possible. In fact, Izzy didn't think she could wait to get married until the autumn. She never wanted to leave Dom's side again. If she managed to get a date, how did Jay Jay feel about being a bridesmaid twice in one month?

That was more difficult.

Jemima took herself to task. She was glad her sister was happy. Of course she was. Okay, she couldn't help the cold breath of loneliness that brushed her when she read Izzy's bubbling message. But she could keep that from Izzy. And what did it matter if Izzy married this month or in August? One day—and soon—she was going to leave the shared apartment and go and live with her Dom and raise little Arctic explorers.

She nibbled a fingernail, trying out replies that wouldn't commit her and at the same time wouldn't spoil Izzy's happiness. It was hopeless. In the end she gave up and wrote, 'As long as you don't want me to wear rose-pink, I'm up for anything.'

And then there were the messages from Basil. She knew

the various aliases he used by now. She zapped them all, unread.

All the other stuff could have waited, really. But she wanted to give Niall Blackthorne time to move on out of the lobby. So she sent chatty replies to a photographer, a charity organiser, a couple of journalists. All of them would be very surprised, she thought wryly.

She copied them to Abby at the PR company—'Look at me being nice to people. Hope it knocks the spoilt brat thing on the head. See you when I get back. Love, J.'

And after that she couldn't think of any more reasons to stay in the office. So she logged off, tidied the desk and the shelves to pristine standard and went cautiously out into the lobby again.

Niall was still there, propped up against the desk and chatting to Al as if he was ready to stay there all day.

Jemima lurked behind the palm tree. She felt faintly ridiculous. But she had won the last bout, she thought wryly. She did not want to push her luck. After all, she had it on good authority that women let Niall Blackthorne get away with murder! And there was nothing to say that she was immune to that charm that Al envied. In fact, there was quite a lot to prove that she wasn't.

So she hovered behind the plants, hoping against hope that he would finish his conversation and go. And then she began to notice the conversation that drifted across the lobby towards her

'Plunging deep at the casino, Niall?'

'Nothing I haven't planned for.'

Al looked at his friend searchingly. 'Sure?'

Niall was serene. 'I'm not worried.'

'Well, if you say so.' Al was relieved, but still curious. 'So what were you doing last night, brooding out there in the dark?'

Jemima tensed. Had someone seen them walking in the moonlight?

Niall sounded faintly puzzled. 'Brooding?'

'You got rid of the dinner jacket and sat on the dock until three. According to Sherlock Holmes in the kitchen, anyway.'

'Ah. The eyes of the world were upon me. What did Primrose think I was doing? Telling over my sins?' Niall's voice was full of laughter.

Al was caustic. 'Plenty to tell, I hear.'

'Gossip,' said Niall reprovingly. But there was that note of laughter in his voice which Jemima was beginning to recognise.

She recognised it because it sent tingles up and down her spine that had absolutely nothing to do with scented breezes or moonlight. Damn it.

'No, not just Primrose's highly coloured gossip. For once.' Al didn't sound as if he took it very seriously, though. 'I've spent too much time this week mopping up a teenager with a crushed crush,' Al added severely. 'Do you *have* to break the heart of every woman you meet here?'

Niall sent his friend an incredulous look. 'You're *complaining*? As a responsible hotelier, you'd have been in a lot more trouble if I'd taken that one up on her offer.'

'Maybe, but—'

'No maybe about it. They can be very determined at seventeen. I had to get one of the maids to frogmarch her out of my cottage on Monday afternoon. Did Primrose tell you that?'

'I heard.' Al's disapproval slipped a bit. 'Why don't nubile blondes come looking for me with champagne and trouble in mind?' he said wistfully.

Niall chuckled. 'Because you're the head honcho and a responsible citizen. Also married.'

'And you're a born lust object, I suppose?' Al was disgusted.

'They think I'm a man of mystery,' said Niall coolly.

Al hooted.

'They think you're James Bond. You turn up at the casino in a white mess jacket and play blackjack until four in the morning,' said Al with irony. 'Or you do usually.' He broke off, as if a thought had just occurred to him. 'I've never heard of you wasting good gambling time sitting on the dock in the moonlight before. Or not alone, anyway. Did she turn you down?'

Niall straightened and looked at the big watch on his muscular wrist. 'Time I was off. Do you want anything in town?'

Al ignored that. 'She did, didn't she?'

Niall said wearily, 'You should try minding your own business some time, Al.'

Al ignored that too. 'Oh wow. You took the backpack brat on the razz and she wasn't dazzled. That *has* to be a first.'

Jemima winced. *The backpack brat!* Was that what they called her? A slow anger started to burn.

Al thought Niall Blackthorne was a charmer? Well, she'd been charmed by the best. He would have to work hard to come up to her standards. In fact, he'd have to work *very* hard. She owed it to her own self-respect. And to half the women in the Caribbean, by the sound of it.

She burst out from behind her palm tree, eyes glittering and vulpine smile firmly in place.

'Oh, good. You're still here,' she told Niall. 'I've changed my mind. You can take me to town after all.'

He was not a fool. His eyebrows flew up and he looked more than a little wary.

But he was no coward either. In fact, she had a sneaking suspicion that he was engaged in some elemental duel with her that they were the only people to recognise. And he was determined to win.

His lips twitched. 'My lucky day,' he said gravely.

Jemima was dry. 'Don't get carried away. All I need is a lift.'

'Then I guess I should be grateful for that.' But he didn't sound grateful. He sounded amused and intrigued—and just a little piqued.

The duel was definitely still in progress.

But he let her out in the market square of Queen's Town when she told him to.

'I'll be down at the dock if you change your mind,' he said, leaning back to watch her as she fumbled with the awkward catch on the door. 'Left at the pirate's statue brings you out onto the waterfront. There aren't any gates or anything. Just wander along beside the moorings until you find me.'

'Sure,' said Jemima, not meaning it.

She jumped down and banged the door shut behind her. She half expected Niall to try and persuade her. But he didn't. Instead he raised a hand in farewell, pushed dark glasses up his nose, and swung the big vehicle away at speed.

Queen's Town turned out to be as tiny as the airport. Its main square had a couple of ramshackle eighteenth-century buildings with pretty ironwork balconies, and there was a handsome customs house on the seafront. Every shop was stocked to the ceiling with stuff that would have been great for fishermen or housewives, or even deep-sea divers. But none of it was much use to Jemima.

In the end she gave up. In spite of herself—or was it what she had secretly wanted to do all along?—she wandered along the waterfront.

It was as hot as a baker's kitchen. The air was full of the scents of exotic fruit and warm bread and coffee—and seaweed and gasoline, she thought with a grimace. There were plenty of people about but nobody hurried.

Boats were unloading. Jemima saw fish of all colours—pearl and silver and inky-blue and orange. There were baskets of tomatoes, plump as piglets, golden corn bursting out of its restraining husk; aubergine gleaming an imperial purple so rich that they looked like part of the Crown Jewels, not something you could slice and eat, and small green sugar apples that looked as if they had just been delivered from Fabergé's factory.

Jemima gave a great sigh of pleasure and bought herself a coffee from a street trader who was happy to take dollars for the paper cup of dark, sweet liquid. She perched on the sea wall, watching the latecoming small boats tie up and start to disgorge their goods. The stone was warm and the salt air was hot against her neck. She put up a hand to protect the skin—and heard her name.

She looked up.

Niall was standing on the deck of a boat, moored at some grey stone steps. He looked exactly as she had had him in her head for the last twenty-four hours—tough, competent, relaxed. *In control.* Unlike her.

He had pushed his sunglasses up on top of his head. Their eyes met. His flared before he could master himself. Not so controlled, then.

Paradoxically, that made her feel even more uncertain. The duel was still on—but neither of them was quite sure where it would end.

Jemima could not make up her mind whether that was a good thing or not. But she found herself standing up and going towards him over the hot cobbles, as if her dusty feet had a mind of their own.

She stopped just out of reach, hardly noticing the interested crew behind him.

He stood easily on the rocking deck. He had discarded his shirt and his skin gleamed in the sun like all the richness of fruit and vegetables being traded behind her.

Jemima swallowed. 'Hi.'

The nearly ugly face was still. 'Going to give me another chance after all?'

She steadied her breathing deliberately before she spoke. 'Depends on what you're offering.'

Oh, that was good, she thought. It sounded upbeat, even amused. At least it sounded as if she had not made a complete pillock of herself every time they were face to face. That had to be a good start.

Niall leaped lightly down from the side of the boat onto the pavement. 'Let's talk about that.'

Jemima tensed. But he did not touch her. Instead he stood in front of her, searching her face as if he did not quite believe what she said. Or that she was here.

Shrewd of him, she thought. It was becoming increasingly difficult to remind herself to be cynical. Suddenly she wished, passionately, that she had been honest with this man.

She looked away before conscience undermined her and she told him her real name.

'Okay. Make your pitch.'

He struck the pose of a Restoration seducer. He could have been the pirate on that statue in the main square. *Careful,* said her inner radio. *This man is sex on a stick. And he knows it.*

He gave her a real seducer's smile too, straight into her eyes so that she almost staggered at the intensity. 'What do you say to a day on a desert island?' he suggested softly.

Jemima blinked. 'What?'

He laughed. Oh, he was gorgeous when he laughed. 'Let me show you a genuine uninhabited island. It's only about two hours' sailing.'

She looked at the boat behind him. 'Is that where they do the scuba diving classes?'

Niall looked at her steadily. 'No. No classes. No crew. I do the sailing. We go alone.'

Jemima's heart did an extreme yo-yo. A whole day alone with him in the middle of the Caribbean? Could she trust him?

Could she trust herself?

'Or we can sign up for scuba on the reef with the guys.'

So she was off the hook. If she wanted to be. Suddenly her inner radio coughed into life again, Madame President on the air. *You have no life. You don't date. You don't go out anywhere unless it's an assignment.*

Suddenly Jemima thought, No life, huh? I'll show her. I'll even show this piratical renegade. I'll show them all.

She threw back her head and gave him a dazzling smile.

'If I can find somewhere to buy swimming things, then I'm all yours.'

His brows flew up. 'Then I shall find you a swimsuit,' he said with a mock bow. 'And let the adventure begin.'

But there was something in his eyes that made her think he meant it. It was exhilarating.

'Okay,' she said. 'Where? I've found high-factor sun-cream in the dive shop, and a sunhat in the ironmongers. But the only swimsuits I've found would go round me twice.'

His eyes gleamed. 'A quest! Trust me. You shall have your swimsuit.'

He seized her by the hand and rushed her across the road into the covered market. It was cooler, but a whole lot nois-ier. He took her straight to a stall that was full of brilliant colours—jewel-coloured silken saris, day-glo batik, embroi-dered cotton shirts.

'This,' he said, almost at once, and flicked a turquoise and cerise bikini out from among the rainbow jumble.

Jemima blinked. The last bikinis she had worn were for a high fashion shoot—black and cream and tawny, deco-rated with gold chains and filmy silk wraps. She had re-clined in a Moorish courtyard, wearing four-inch heels, while the photographer draped her and the material this way and that in the sun. Not one of those swimsuits, she was certain, would have survived a serious swim.

These colours hurt her eyes, but the bikinis looked sturdy enough to build a road in. Only a few had a price tag. Not one of them had a size indicator in it.

She laughed suddenly. Jemima Dare wearing a twenty-dollar bikini! She would have to remember to tell the PR people about that. She put her head on one side, assess-ing them.

'This one,' she said, accepting his colour scheme but re-placing it with a more realistic size.

He paid for it while she was still fumbling with her purse. And she found he had thrown in a sarong in shades of lapis lazuli and sea-blue and a severely practical pair of khaki shorts.

'You shouldn't,' she said, as awkward as a teenager with her first boyfriend. 'No one has bought clothes for me since I was a kid.'

His eyes flicked down her. She felt herself go hot.

'Then savour the new experience,' he said lightly.

But his eyes weren't light.

Jemima swallowed and looked away. 'I—er—I may need some more sunblock. If we're going to be out in the sun all day.'

Ethereal pallor was her trademark. She could not afford to go back to London with an unscheduled tan, she thought, grinning. She had a photo shoot next week.

But today was hers, and hers alone.

'Over there,' he said, waving her towards another stall.

She bought some aloe moisturiser as well, and a pair of big sunglasses. When she joined him on the quay again Niall was carrying a couple of grocery sacks and climbing nimbly into the boat. The other crew members had disappeared.

He put his burden down and held out a hand.

Jemima scrambled onto the boat, grateful for it. She nodded at the bag. 'Stocking up for a week?'

His eyes gleamed. 'Don't worry. I have to be back to-night. Don't forget, that's when I go to work.'

She stirred the brown bag with her foot. 'So what's all this?'

'The makings of a picnic. A couple of things you might need.'

'Me?' She was wary. Not alarmed. She was an experi-enced woman who had been chatted up in four continents, she reminded herself. Certainly not alarmed. Just—careful. 'You've bought me a present? Another present?'

He leaned forward and gazed deep into her eyes, like Casanova on the case.

'Just a little something to wear. I had to guess the size.'

'Something else to wear?' She felt her cheeks were on fire. And, sophisticate or no, her voice rose in a squeak of pure alarm.

She sounded like a chipmunk in a panic, she thought disgustedly. But she couldn't help it.

He straightened, pleased.

'Here.' And from the second brown paper bag he produced a pair of floppy black rubber pumps.

Jemima took them like an automaton. They looked like lifeless fish.

'What on earth—?'

'Sea urchins.' And when she looked even more blank he said blandly, 'Nasty little spiny animals. I told you last night. You can't go staggering about the beach on heels. But you can't go barefoot. Sea urchins are everywhere, and much too easy to tread on. They're painful and they can turn septic, too. So—you wear these to wander about. In fact, you should wear them when you're swimming too.'

'Th-thank you.'

His eyes crinkled up. 'We aim to please.'

He's irresistible, thought Jemima suddenly.

From the quiet smile that played about his mouth she suspected he knew it.

But he did not push his advantage. Instead, he gave her a brisk guided tour of the boat and set about making ready.

She had been right about the competence, Jemima saw. He hoisted sail and took the little boat out into the harbour with a calm expertise which did nothing to hide his enjoyment. Once they were out in the open sea he came and sat beside her, his face tilted to the sun.

'Great, isn't it?'

They were not far from land yet, but even so in open water there was a breeze. It ruffled his dark hair, making him look even more like one of the island's piratical settlers.

Jemima watched with appreciation. 'You do this a lot?'

'Do what? Carry off unsuspecting women? Or sail?'

Their eyes met. She narrowed hers. 'Sail. I'm not unsuspecting. I can take care of myself.'

He laughed. 'Good.'

She could not interpret that. 'So you sail regularly?'

The breeze shifted a little. He got up to adjust the sail. Without his shirt, it was clear that he was unexpectedly muscular. These were not the over-developed abs of the glamorous male models she worked with, though. These were muscles he needed—and used.

Oh, yes, he was irresistible all right. She had never met anyone like him.

He narrowed his eyes at the horizon, then looked up the mast.

'Regularly?' He sounded absent. 'No, not these days. I sailed all the time when I was a boy. We had a lake in one direction and the Gulf Stream in the other. I learned to sail when other kids were getting their first bicycle.'

Jemima looked at the way he moved with the lift and fall of the boat and was not surprised. He trimmed the sail, then sat down next to her again, one arm thrown casually behind her.

She leaned forward. 'Were you born on Pentecost?'

Niall looked completely blank for a moment. 'On the island? No. What makes you think that?'

She looked round the perfect little deck. 'Your boat.'

'Oh, that. Not mine, I'm afraid. I borrowed her from the guys. I don't have a boat of my own any more. Not in Pentecost or anywhere else.'

Was that a note of regret in his voice? She did not think he was a man given to regret. He would think it a waste of time. She was sure of it.

Still, she wanted to know more about him. 'Why not? Too expensive?'

He shrugged. 'Lifestyle, I suppose you'd call it. I travel

all the time. If you live out of a suitcase, you don't have
anywhere to moor a boat.'

Or a home, thought Jemima. It sounded bleak.

'Did you choose to be a nomad?'

He scanned the ocean. 'In a way.'

She said nothing.

He looked down at her. 'You want to know the full story
of my scandalous life?'

Yes!

But there was still that duel. She shrugged as if she didn't
care. But it left the door open for confidences if he wanted…
She hoped—oh, how she hoped—that he wanted…

'Okay, then.' He stretched. 'I ran away from home when
I was seventeen.'

For some reason that shocked her. '*Ran away?* Were you
badly treated?'

He chuckled. 'Well, they didn't send me up chimneys, if
that's what you mean. But it had been coming a long time.
I had a blazing row with the current stepmother. And my
brother thought he could ground me. I told them both to
stuff it. Stole the kitchen float. And walked out.'

Jemima frowned. This did not sound like any family life
she knew anything about. 'Your brother grounded you?
What happened to your father?'

'Off getting another divorce. Though none of us knew
that at the time.' He laughed at her expression. 'Don't look
so appalled. We were the original dysfunctional family.'

'It sounds as if you were better off without them,' she
said, oddly furious for him.

Well, for the seventeen-year-old he had been, she assured
herself. Tears pricked at the back of her eyes. It unsettled
her.

'Oh, one or two of the stepmothers were okay. My
brother, though—what a complete bastard. Very like my
father in lots of ways.'

Jemima found that she could have cried quite easily.
Which was crazy. His reminiscences had not disturbed Niall

at all. She wished she had bought a handkerchief as well as
a hat, and tried to sniff quietly. It was not a success.

'Hey.' He put a hand under her chin and turned her face
to him. He was laughing. 'No need to look like that. It's a
long time ago.'

'I'm not,' she said, not very coherently. 'It's just that I
love my parents, and I have this great sister, and I think it's
a shame when families hate each other.'

She had to sniff again. No point in trying to hide it, with
him watching her like that. She scrubbed the back of her
hand across her face.

'I need a tissue,' she said disagreeably.

He tossed her canvas bag across to her. She caught it and
rootled until she found a scrap of paper handkerchief that
had seen better days. She blew her nose savagely.

'Hey,' he said again, more gently.

She pulled herself together. It was stupid to go spraying
unwanted sympathy around.

'I suppose you don't see them any more?'

'Haven't been home in over fifteen years,' he agreed
cheerfully. 'My father died and my brother— well, have you
heard of the English habit of having an heir and a spare?'

'What?'

'If you wanted to pass on an estate to your descendants
you had the son and heir, who was going to cop the lot, and
then you had another son as an insurance policy, in case the
first one got the plague. Well, I'm the spare.'

It sounded dreadful. Jemima said so, before she had time
to stop herself.

'Depends on the family, I guess,' said Niall tolerantly.
'Not great in ours, I admit. Running away was a real one
in the eye for them.'

She blew her nose again. 'Is that why you became a professional gambler? To annoy your family?'

He had risen to trim the sails again. But at that he looked
over his shoulder, his eyes dancing.

'For a girl with such a wonderful family you seem to have quite a grasp on the politics of hostility.'

'I'd sometimes want to do something that made them really furious,' she admitted. 'Well, for a while anyway. Don't you get tired of it?'

'Ah, but I was born to gamble,' he assured her solemnly. 'I have a photographic memory and I'm ace with numbers. A natural.'

'If you say so.'

But, looking up at him, with the spray leaving diamond droplets on his tanned chest and his eyes narrowed against the dazzling sea, Jemima thought he looked more as if he were born to sail.

'Don't you ever want to do anything else?'

'Oh, one day, maybe.' His tone was dismissive.

Then he began to point out the features of Pentecost's southern coastline and confidences were over.

He kept the travelogue up all the way to the island he had promised her. The only time he stopped talking about the wildlife or geology was when he told her to move or, once, to put on a hat.

And her one successful purchase blew away!

'Oh, damn! No hat now,' said Jemima.

'That's where you're wrong.' He ran lightly down the companionway and re-emerged with a battered straw hat with some ageing cherries pinned to its brim.

'That looks as if it's been sailing the Caribbean longer than either of us has been alive,' said Jemima, startled.

'Don't knock it. It's Ellie's grandmother's gardening hat. I swiped it this morning. You'll need it. The sun is lot stronger in these latitudes than Europeans allow for.'

Jemima accepted the hat philosophically, and rammed it down on top of the tangle that the wind had made of her hair. If the agency could see her now they'd *die*! She bit back a grin.

'It sounds as if you come here a lot, even if you don't live here.'

'I go everywhere there's blackjack,' he said dryly. 'Didn't I tell you last night? From Las Vegas to London. From New Jersey to Monaco. '

Jemima was ultra-casual. 'I live in London.'

He raised those wicked eyebrows. 'And I had you down for another nomad.'

'Me?' She was astonished. 'No! Why?'

'Travelling alone. Minimal luggage. Don't bother to book a hotel in advance. You're not the run-of-the-mill tourist.'

There was something in his voice which made her look at him sharply.

He added softly, 'And you don't like people carrying your bags.'

'What?'

'Like to keep it in your hands. Got something precious in it, has it? A file? Some press cuttings?' His voice was still lazy, but somehow it sounded as if he was interrogating her and it was important.

Jemima shook her head. 'No. Nothing like that.'

'So you didn't come to Pentecost on an assignment?'

She gave a crack of laughter. 'Far from it. I suppose I've run away, just as much as you did.'

He searched her face. 'Run away?' he echoed, as if he did not believe her.

There was a little gust of wind that blew a strand of red-gold hair across her lips. It lifted the disgraceful hat. Jemima grabbed it and held it in place, squinting up at him.

'Oh, yes,' she said, admitting it at last. 'There was something I couldn't handle and I turned tail.' She grimaced. 'Not very impressive.'

He waited. When she did not go on he said, 'But you live in London? Probably have a regular job, too?'

She bit back a smile. 'Well, fairly regular.'

He sent her a quick look. 'Are you going to tell me what that means?'

She jumped. 'What?'

'The private laughter.'

All amusement died abruptly. Jemima's eyes widened. She shifted on her wooden seat.

'You're very sharp,' she said at last.

'Part of my stock in trade, reading people. I'm an expert on body language.'

That made her feel even more uneasy.

'Can you read me?'

He gave the ghost of a laugh. 'Up to a point,' he said.

He wouldn't be drawn any further, no matter how much she tried to beguile him.

So she kicked off her shoes, wedged the hat on her head more firmly, and gave herself up to enjoyment.

The sea was like a great animal, purring with pleasure because they had come to play, she thought. Around them it was no colour, but as it stretched to the horizon it was blue and purple and even turquoise, where it curled round an island. Above them the sky was cloudless aquamarine. When Jemima half closed her eyes, the sun struck rainbows off the mast. A faint breeze cooled her skin deliciously. High in the bright sky great birds wheeled with majestic slowness.

'It's like a dream,' said Jemima, stretching luxuriously.

Niall was busy at the helm, but at that he looked across at her and grinned.

'With our own desert island waiting for us,' he said in thrilling voice. 'No buildings, no people, no electricity. Just us and the elements.'

'Mmm. Sounds like heaven.'

'Of course that means we have to catch our own food, build our own cooking fire, dig our own poo pit…'

Jemima waved a lazy hand. 'I don't care. I can handle it.'

'You think?'

She tipped back and looked up at the birds. Their great wings spread, they seemed just to lie on the thermal up-drafts, abandoning themselves to the power of the elements. And the wind took care of them.

I want to be like that.

'Yup,' she told the sky with confidence. 'For a day in Paradise, I can handle anything.'

The movement of the sea around them seemed to change. She sat up and saw that they were really getting quite close to one of the islands. Niall stopped teasing and began to concentrate.

The shoreline looked impenetrable to Jemima, with vertical swathes of rock and densely wooded hillside tumbling straight into the sea. Only then they rounded a headland, and she drew a long breath in sheer wonder.

It was a natural harbour. The water was as clear as aquamarines at a beauty's throat. It pawed at the pristine sand like a lazy cat—stretch and withdraw, stretch and withdraw. Will I be bothered to do it again? Yeah, why not? Stretch even further, slower...and withdraw.

'It's perfect,' said Jemima softly.

Niall lowered the sail and they drifted in with the current, on a curving trajectory that took them the length of the empty beach.

At first all Jemima could see were great dark trees that looked as if they would be more at home in the jungle. The beach below them was deeply shaded, and a steep green slope rose up behind them.

'Mangroves,' said Niall, working the rudder with effortless expertise. 'There's a stream comes into the sea there. We get fresh water from it if we run out of bottled stuff.'

Beyond the mangroves the beach flattened out and the vegetation became sparse. At the far end there was a scattering of smooth rocks. Niall nosed the boat into the lea of the rock shelf and dropped anchor. Then he jumped out and turned to give Jemima a hand.

But she had already jumped after him. The water came up to her thighs and made her stagger. He caught her strongly and held on. The water lapped and swirled about her. But in the passionless embrace she felt utterly stable.

She let herself sway with the water, laughing, as she turned to look round the beach in amazement.

'It's like something out of a children's adventure book.'

There was an avenue of palm trees, like great open fans, where the beach met the grassy scrub. The sand was as smooth as a bowl of newly sifted flour.

'And there's nobody here but us,' she said softly, wonderingly.

'Told you.'

She stood very still. She was aware of the dense, living matter of the ocean floor under her bare feet, of the tang of salt, of the cicadas crackling incessantly in the trees, the steady swish, swish of the tide.

And, under it all, the *silence*.

Jemima's lips parted. 'It's real. It really is.'

'You'd better believe it.'

For some reason tears seemed to be stinging her eyes. She shook her head impatiently.

Niall looked down at her. Suddenly the nearly ugly features seemed to be the handsomest, kindest, most vital she had ever seen. He scanned her face for a moment. Then slowly, as if it was terribly important and he wanted to do it *right*, he put out a gentle hand and, scarcely moving at all, stroked a strand of windblown hair off her face. It felt as if all the warmth and strength in the world was there, just waiting for her to…to…to…

To do what? Say what? Jemima didn't know. All those parties, all those glamorous men and that sophisticated flirtation and she had no idea what to do next.

She stood as still as a woman in a dream. Off balance. Dazzled. Desperately confused. And—somehow—incredibly shy.

The brown hand cupping her head stilled. Dark eyes searched her face. There was no longer a vestige of teasing in them.

'You shall have your day in Paradise,' he said, very low, almost fierce. 'Trust me.'

It was a vow.

CHAPTER SIX

THEY splashed to shore, hand in hand, laughing.

For a moment Jemima thought of the couples she had seen last night, hand in hand. Of Izzy and Dom, her parents. Hand in hand meant, I love you. We are together. Well, it did for everyone else.

But Niall Blackthorne was a stranger. He didn't love her. He thought she was fun and sexy and knew the score. And she was. She was. She wished she wasn't. She wished she were an innocent for whom walking hand in hand meant something.

Well, there was no point in thinking about that now. The place was magic. The man was gorgeous. And there was adventure in the air.

'First footprints!' said Jemima gaily. 'I can't resist.'

She danced on the spot, laughing at him. He let go her hand.

The sand was as hot as freshly cooked toast under her bare feet. She gave a wild whoop and pounded off along the beach. Silky sand flew under her heels. Once she was out of the lee of the rocks it was almost too hot to bear, but she kept on running.

In the end she tumbled onto the ground under a low branching tree at the edge of the beach and looked back. Niall was standing watching her, his face alight with laughter. Between them stretched a straight line of footprints. He gave her a mock salute.

She waved energetically, beckoning.

'That's some battle cry you've got,' he said, as he strolled up. 'You could train rugby teams.'

Jemima grinned. 'I'll take that as a compliment,' she said sedately.

He slipped a strap off his shoulder and she realised that he had been carrying a substantial bag.

'What's in there?'

'Beer.'

She hooted. 'That's a very masculine idea of an ideal picnic.'

'And your bikini. And my snorkel. And—' He brought out a long blade. Even in its leather sheath it looked wicked.

Jemima gasped. 'What's that, for heaven's sake? A cutlass?'

'A machete,' said Niall calmly.

'You own a machete?' Her voice rose to a squawk.

'No, I borrowed it from Al. But I know how to use it, don't worry.'

She collapsed back onto the lacy shadowed sand.

'I'm alone with an axe murderer,' she told the blazing sky dramatically.

Niall stayed calm. 'This thing only murders breadfruit and mangoes.'

But Jemima was enjoying herself too much to stop teasing. 'You're going to ravish me and then make me become a pirate like you,' she announced.

Niall nodded enthusiastically. 'That sounds like fun.'

She turned tragic eyes on him. 'I shall end up walking the plank and never see my family again.'

'Ah, but think of all those life experiences. You might even end up a pirate in your own right.' He was rummaging through the bag and threw the new bikini at her. 'If you have the talent. Of course, you need to be a really *bad* girl.'

Jemima caught the day-glo scraps of fabric neatly. 'Ah, then I'll never make the grade,' she said, disappointed. 'I've been a good girl all my life.'

Niall looked up, arrested His eyes gleamed.

'Stick with me, kid,' he growled. 'I'll show you the ropes.'

And before she could say a word, or even take a breath, he bent and kissed her.

It was a hard kiss, fast and fleeting. It could have been casual. It could have been half a joke, still part of the pirate game.

But it wasn't. Jemima knew it wasn't. Although Niall turned away at once and continued to unpack the bag without saying a thing. She could still feel the pressure on her mouth. The pressure was more eloquent than any words.

It said— We're equals. I want you. Now you know it.

Yes, she knew it. Knew it more clearly than she could ever remember doing before. But did she know what she wanted to do about it? Not for a moment.

Sobered, Jemima sat up and started to help him unpack.

'Shoes,' he said, tossing across the pair that he had shown her on the boat. 'Keep them on. We're a long way from the nearest doctor if you tread on a sea urchin.'

She did not argue. 'Thank you,' she said quietly, and slipped them on.

She did not want him to touch her again, not while she was in such turmoil. And he didn't. Without being told.

Instead he said, 'Come and see our island.'

Relieved, she got to her feet. 'You've been here before, then?'

He smiled. 'Yes. Sorry. There have been footprints before yours.'

'But it is uninhabited?'

'Oh, yes. Not a McDonalds in sight. We pick and catch our food. In fact, we'd better get started.' He took an empty can out of the bag. 'Fresh water,' he explained, when she looked surprised. 'I don't expect my dates to drink nothing but warm beer.'

His date! It felt as if he was laying claim to her in a couple of negligent syllables.

Jemima remembered Al's amused accusations. The man cut a swathe through the female guests! They let him get away with murder! Be careful, she told her tremulous heart.

You may think you're sophisticated. But this man is way, way out of your territory.

She followed him, a faint frown between her brows. Niall did not seem to notice.

He clearly knew the island well. He pointed out mango trees only a few minutes from the beach,

'We'll pick some up on the way back.'

Once away from the shore, they plunged among dense trees, and the land grew steep.

'Can I hear a stream?' Jemima asked.

'You've got good ears. Yes.'

Niall was utterly impersonal. She was grateful for it. She was almost sure she was grateful.

'So this is where we get water?'

He kept up a steady pace. 'A bit further up. The stream runs over rocks there. It's muddy down here.'

Jemima bent forward. 'I didn't realise it would be such a climb,' she said, trying hard not to sound breathless. Niall was breathing as easily as if they were still rolling along the beach. In case he thought she couldn't keep up, she added hastily, 'Or that there would be so many trees.'

Niall didn't halt, but he did slow down a little. 'This should all be jungle,' he said. 'Only the sea level changed and drowned all but the peaks. You have real Amazon banyan trees here, if you know where to look. The locals say the jungle devils live in them.'

'And you do know where to look?'

He nodded.

'But I thought you were just a visitor,' she said slowly. 'You sound like a long-term resident.'

He shrugged. 'I like to know about the places I stay.'

She considered that. 'To the point of tracking down your own deserted corner of Amazon jungle? Like marking some territory for yourself?'

He gave a startled snort of laughter. 'You're very shrewd.'

But he didn't sound too pleased about it.

Jemima said curiously, 'Do you really travel from casino to casino all the time? Don't you have a home of any kind? Anywhere?'

He shook his head. 'Not really.'

'But where do you keep your books, your music?'

He smiled. 'I buy books at airports and leave them in hotel rooms. I have a Walkman and five CDs. I'm not a natural nest-builder.'

'But where do people send you letters?'

'That's what e-mail is for.'

Jemima thought about it. They were still climbing.

'What about birthday presents?' she said triumphantly.

'There's no one who would send me a birthday present,' he said indifferently.

She was honestly appalled. 'That's terrible.'

'No, it isn't. I don't get a lot of useless tat I don't want and would have to waste time writing thank-you letters for. And nobody expects a birthday present back from me.'

The bleakness of it silenced her.

But then he stopped in front of a tree and looked up into the branches.

'Breadfruit,' he said in congratulatory tones. 'Stand still. Now you will see the wonders of the machete.'

He hacked down a fruit the size and shape of a football. He sniffed it.

'Overripe. Oh, well, it may cook all right. Anyway, it will be an experience for you.'

'One of many,' muttered Jemima.

Niall did not answer that. He pulled a string bag arrangement out of his pocket, slipped it round the fruit and slung it over his shoulder. Then he turned downhill. An overgrown path led to a small waterfall. He uncapped the water carrier and held it under the stream.

Jemima hung back a little, watching and listening.

The water gurgled and gushed round slabs of what looked like granite. The air was full of squeaks and trills and the sound of small animals scampering, though the cicadas were not so insistent up here. There was a smell of vegetation, and something heavy and sweet like lilies. It felt very still and strange.

Instinctively Jemima moved closer to Niall.

He was putting the cap back on the water carrier, but he looked up at that.

'You okay?'

'This place—' She tried to put her unease into words. 'It makes me feel very small. And sort of impermanent.'

'You're fine as long as you stay on the path.'

'I suppose so.'

He stood up. 'I'll take care of you.' He said it kindly, but it was quite impersonal.

And suddenly Jemima didn't want him impersonal any more. She wanted him concerned and protective and… and…

And piratical. Admit it, Jemima. You want the big production number. Swept up into his arms and carried off aboard his ship. That's what you're after. What an idiot you are.

She swallowed. 'Of course you will,' she said in her coolest voice. 'I just had a wobble for a moment. I'll be fine.'

They went down to the beach a whole lot faster than they had come up. By the time they came in sight of their little tree, with its lacework of dappled shadows, she was almost running.

'I want to swim,' she said.

She turned her back on him and scrambled into the bikini without letting herself think about it. And then she ran into the sea as if all the jungle devils were after her.

She half thought Niall would follow her. But he did not. She didn't know whether to be glad or affronted. And then she forgot her equivocal feelings in the sheer pleasure of swimming in sea like warm silk.

Jemima had always been a strong swimmer. This water, with its gentle swell and startling clarity, was no effort at all. She did several lengths of the beach in a strong fast crawl. And slowly, slowly, all the agitation dissolved.

Niall Blackthorne was a sexy stranger and she didn't read him very well; that was all. It was no big deal. She didn't need to feel as if her whole world was turning upside down. If he touched her again she could handle it. And if he didn't—well, she could handle that too.

Calm again, Jemima allowed herself to play for a while. She turned somersaults, then dived deep, as far as her breath would take her, and came up spluttering. She swam along just under the surface, among jewel-coloured fish who swam round her curiously, surfacing from time to time to take another long breath.

She kept checking her distance from the shore. Sometimes when he saw her looking Niall waved. But he did not join her.

Eventually, even Jemima had to admit she was tired. She swam to shore with lazy strokes and trod wearily up the beach.

But she still said, 'That was wonderful,' as she flopped down on the sand.

Niall, she found, had built a small bonfire of twigs and driftwood and was now stretched out in the shade, his shirt bunched under his head.

Jemima averted her eyes from his alluring bare chest and said brightly, 'Got the boy scout's badge for making a fire, did you?'

He chuckled. 'Oh, I did the full woodsman's thing.'

'Congratulations. And we need a fire why?'

'Barbecue,' he said briefly. 'When you're hungry I'll go catch a fish.'

Jemima shook her head, revolted. 'Absolutely not. I've just been swimming with those fish. They're my friends.'

There was a moment's disbelieving silence. Then he flung back his head and laughed until he choked.

She glared, mock affronted. At least she hoped it was

mock. She didn't want to turn into an over-sensitive wimp, not with unpredictable Niall Blackthorne.

When he stopped laughing, he said, 'Just as well I did bring some food from the market, then.'

Jemima narrowed her eyes at him and made a discovery. 'You've been winding me up. You never meant us to live off the land today.'

His eyes danced. 'Let's just say I brought some insurance.'

The insurance was a deliciously sweet lettuce, avocados, tomatoes, a cold chicken and a great bunch of bananas. Jemima ate with relish and washed it down with the sweet water they had collected from the stream.

'Wonderful. Though it's a shame to waste your fire.'

He was sitting cross-legged, all mahogany skin and vitality. He shrugged those strong shoulders and Jemima caught her breath. She turned it into a cough.

'Sorry about that,' she said with determined lightness.

'Don't worry about it. Someone else will land and use the fire eventually.'

She pulled a face. 'You mean someone less squeamish than me?'

He smiled suddenly. It made his eyes crinkle up at the corners. It was unnervingly sexy. She looked away before he could read her thoughts.

'I like you for being squeamish,' he said. 'If striped sticklebacks are your friends, you should stand up and admit it.'

Jemima sighed. 'You think I'm awfully girly, don't you?'

His eyes darkened. Very unnervingly sexy. He shook his head. 'You don't want to know what I think.'

'Go on. I can take it,' she said dryly.

'Can you? Sure about that?'

Their eyes locked. She could not tear her gaze away. And she felt all her defences crumble. Against him, against herself—they all turned to water and leaked away into the great sunny ocean behind his head. Every last weapon in her armoury melted—the wry self-mockery, the teasing, defensive laughter. Last to go was the sophistication. After years of the worst that the fashion industry could throw at her she would have said that she could handle any man in the world. But that went too. It left her felt naked and bewildered.

And vulnerable.

'Can you, indeed?' said Niall Blackthorne.

And took her in his arms.

It was like walking off the world. Jemima's head fell back. Her eyes closed as if the air was too bright for them.

She became aware of every last atom in her body. They all seemed to be quivering. Heat engulfed her. Heat and the sense of sheer physical power—his, her own. She put her newly charged hands on his shoulders and felt the electricity surge through him.

She thought, *He's out of control. That makes two of us.*

They fell to the sand, locked and breathless. She heard his heart. It seemed to be slamming through her body too. How could a simple kiss seem this *big*?

Except, of course, it wasn't a simple kiss. It was a journey to the furthest galaxy. It was a probe into the core of her being. When their lips parted she was changed.

Niall raised himself off her. He shook his head, laughing a little, as if he were as amazed as she was.

'Wow,' was all he said. But Jemima knew what he meant.

She meant it too. She could feel a smile breaking through, bursting out like a butterfly out of a chrysalis. Wholly new. Entirely *gorgeous*.

'Wow to you too.' She could hardly stop herself from laughing with delight.

He touched her lips. His mahogany-brown arm was covered with a fine dusting of sand. She ran her fingers along it in wonder, barely touching his skin.

'You look frosted.'

He shivered under her touch. But his voice was still that laughing Niall voice she would know, now, in her heart's core for the rest of her life. 'I don't feel frosted,' he said dryly.

Jemima gave a hiccup of startled amusement. 'No, you don't,' she agreed appreciatively. She mimed a kiss.

His eyes went black. He hauled her against him again, as if he could not bear even that tiny distance between them. This time it was she who kissed him. They were sticky with sand and sweat and salt from the sea water, but it made no difference. She wanted him. Needed him as she had never needed anything or anyone.

And it was mutual. Even out of control and starving, she knew that. His body told her.

He raised his head. 'Let's go back to the boat.' It was not much more than a gasp.

'What?' In her frenzy, Jemima was not sure she had heard him properly.

'The boat. Now.'

'*No.*' She could not believe that he could even contemplate not touching her, even for a moment. She ran a voluptuous hand over his thigh. 'You don't mean that.'

He groaned. 'Jay Jay—'

She wriggled under him. It was deliberate. 'Do you?'

He caught her hand and rolled off her. He caught her other hand and held it between them, his chest heaving.

'I want to make love.' His voice was rough. 'Properly. That means protection. No sodding sand. God help me, even a pillow for your head.'

'*Oh.*' She was shaken back to sobriety. But it was a new sort of sobriety, with her blood beating like a steam hammer and her heart full. She could not think of a thing to say.

He dropped his head so that his brow rested against hers.

'Let me take care of you, Jay Jay.' His words were muffled. 'I need to.'

She was shaken by a huge tenderness. She cupped a powdery hand round his head. He was shaking.

'Yes,' she said simply.

They ran back to the boat. Hand in hand again. But this time, thought Jemima, it was real.

On the boat, they dusted sand off each other with grave

ceremony. He brought cushions from below and made a bower for her, out of the sun. Then he peeled her bright bikini away, between kisses. She was rougher with his Bermuda shorts. But she was far out on the ocean of love then, and so was he.

Afterwards, she lay in his arms, feeling bone against bone as she never had before. Feeling complete.

'Amazing,' she said, drifting off to sleep.

She thought he kissed her hair. The famous Titian glory had never looked worse. It was damp and tangled, smelling of sea water and full of sand. And he kissed it!

'This,' she said drowsily, 'is a new experience.'

And slept, feeling loved.

She woke to the smell of coffee. She sat up, rubbing her eyes. She felt as if her whole body was smiling. Still feeling loved, then. This was new, thought Jemima.

She looked round. The sun had moved. The sky had changed. There were a few clouds, away on the horizon.

Niall put his head through the hatch.

'Awake?'

Jemima turned. He was smiling at her. His eyes were clear. The raging intensity was exhausted. But something else had taken its place.

She thought, *You know me now.*

It was like having their first breakfast together. It was like being on an old-fashioned honeymoon. Love again!

She put out a hand to him.

He kissed it, quite unselfconsciously. As if it was the most natural thing in the world. As if he loved her too.

'Coffee?'

'Mmm.'

He brought two mugs of black fragrant coffee onto the deck and lay down beside her. He had put his shorts on again. Jemima plucked at the waistband, making a face.

He shook his head, mock defensive. 'Look, I was messing about with boiling water. A chap has to think of these things.'

'Wimp,' she said peacefully.

He kissed her shoulder. 'Wanton.'

They sipped coffee in perfect harmony.

She said dreamily, 'I think I like boats.'

'They're good things,' he agreed. 'I crewed on a banana boat once. Always wanted to go back.'

'Was that when you ran away from home?'

'Yup.'

'Very glamorous,' she said in congratulatory tones.

He chuckled. 'It makes a great story. I wouldn't want to do it again.'

She snuggled into the curve of his arm. 'Tell me.'

'Tell you what?'

'About being seventeen and running away.'

'Really?' He sounded disconcerted.

'Really.'

He pulled a face. 'Okay. It's nothing very special. I had a big fight with my father. He wanted me to go in the army. I wanted to go to university and study maths. I was good. I mean really good. I don't like waste.'

Jemima was puzzled. 'Couldn't he afford it? Aren't there grants?'

'He could afford it.' Niall was grim. 'That was why I couldn't get a grant. He was getting through money like water then, but he could still have afforded it. He just didn't want to. He and my brother weren't academic and he didn't see why I should be. Younger sons did what they were told.'

Jemima was indignant. 'Bastard.'

He hugged her. 'It was a bit of a bummer at the time. But—every setback is an opportunity. I was good at numbers; I thought I'd make it work for me. I'd been to a couple of casinos on holiday. I thought I could work my way round the world as a croupier. I even had the tuxedo.' His voice was heavy with irony. 'My father would always stump up for stuff he thought was essential.'

Jemima was astonished at her own fury. 'Double bastard.'

He chuckled. 'You got my vote there.'

'So how did you turn from a croupier into a gambler?'

'I didn't make it to croupier. I was too young. That was why I went to the other side of the tables. Meanwhile I worked at anything I could to put bread in my mouth. I've been a waiter, a courier, a meat porter…you name it, I've done it.'

'And sailor on a banana boat.'

'That was one of the good ones.'

She kissed his neck. 'I'm glad.'

He lifted her chin and kissed her mouth sweetly. 'Thank you for being glad.'

She returned his kiss with enthusiasm, until he slid his hand along the long naked length of her. He stopped unexpectedly.

'You're burning. Where's your suncream?'

She pouted. But he was adamant. And she was too lazily content to fight him. She found her bag and fished out the tube.

Niall took it away from her. 'Lie down.'

'What?'

He leered at her wolfishly. 'Captain's perks. Once aboard the lugger and the wench is mine.'

She gave a startled choke of laughter. 'Do you read minds?'

He was uncapping the tube. 'Sorry?'

'That's what I was thinking earlier. Well—wishing, actually. I wanted you to do the full pirate thing. Carry me off and sail into the sunset.'

'You got it.' He kissed her lingeringly. 'Now, lie back and think of England.'

Laughing, she fell back onto the blanket he had spread for her. He started applying the suncream with distracting thoroughness.

Jemima decided it wasn't fair. 'Have you ever been home since?' she asked brightly.

He was lingering over her hipbone. 'Define home.'

That startled her out of her hazy, sexy dream. 'You're not serious?'

Niall started on her legs. 'My father had two sons, three houses, five wives at the last count. I went to boarding school when I was five. Spent holidays with relatives or schoolfriends. I've been living out of a suitcase a long time.'

Jemima was appalled. She jack-knifed into a sitting position and hugged him hard.

'Hey,' said Niall in a muffled voice against her breasts. 'It made me the man I am today. Are you complaining?'

She relaxed her convulsive grip. 'No.'

'Good.' He touched her face. 'Are you crying?' he said, astonished.

She turned her head away. ''Course not.'

He turned her chin gently to face him. 'No one's ever cried over me before. But there's no need, honey. Really. I did fine.'

Jemima swallowed. 'Sure you did.' She sniffed. 'So you don't go back…' She hesitated; 'home' was clearly the wrong word here. '…to the UK? Ever?' Too late she realised how wistful she sounded. Damn it!

Niall let her go and said practically, 'Turn over and I'll do your back.'

Oh, hell, it had sounded as if she wanted a proper relationship. She might just as well have said, Come to London and be my love. Not what you said to a footloose pirate. She had probably blown everything now. Stupid, stupid, *stupid*.

She turned over, grateful to hide her suddenly pink face. She felt the cool cream on her shoulders and tried to think of a way to retrieve her mistake.

Above her, Niall said thoughtfully, 'I go to London sometimes. Too many casinos not to. But I've only been back to one of my childhood hosts once.'

'Oh?'

'It was interesting.' His voice was odd.

Jemima screwed her head round to look at him. His eyes were far away.

'Doesn't sound good,' she said with quick compassion. 'Want to tell me about it?'

He came back to the present with a little jump. 'You,' he said on a startled breath, 'are the sweetest thing I've ever found.'

She sat up and took the cream away from him.

'Tell me.'

He hesitated. 'It's not very distinguished.'

'So?'

His throat moved. 'I was twenty-eight. I thought I knew everything. I'd been everywhere, done everything. I'd never taken a woman seriously.' He looked ashamed. 'And suddenly there she was. ''The not impossible she.'' The one I couldn't walk away from.'

There was sudden total silence. Jemima's hand stilled. She stared and stared at the tube of suncream as if it were a key to another universe. She thought, Well, I asked. Why does it feel as if he just shot me?

She said, very quietly, 'What happened?'

'She wouldn't have me.' Niall's voice was quite expressionless.

'Wouldn't—?' Jemima thought about Al's envy, of all those hungry, bewildered women who let Niall Blackthorne get away with murder, of the way he had made her feel loved. 'She's crazy, right?'

'Very much not. She's a homebody. I haven't had a home since I was seventeen. Never wanted one.' Niall's voice was even. 'But Abigail did. She wanted a home like the one she grew up in.'

'Ah,' said Jemima, understanding at last. 'James Bond wouldn't do, then?'

There was a pause.

Then, 'James Bond's girlfriends all die,' said Niall lightly. 'No woman in her right mind wants James Bond when she stops to think about it.'

I wouldn't mind.

She nearly said it aloud. It was terrifying.

She said crisply, 'I have to tell you that's not an opinion widely shared.'

'Well, not my Abigail, then.'

My Abigail. Would he ever say *My Jay Jay* with that aching longing in his voice? No, of course he wouldn't. She was a sexy amusement for a tropical afternoon. She was crazy if she thought anything else.

His next words confirmed it.

'Women like mystery, right? Or they think they do. Well, Abigail knows me too well to think I'm a man of mystery. And she would hate living on the hoof. She wants cats and dogs and horses. And an estate to keep them on.'

Jemima did not like the sound of the absent Abigail at all. 'Sounds like a gold-digger,' she said crisply.

'No.' Niall's voice was full of tenderness. 'She was brought up on a place like that. She was made for that sort of life. I couldn't give it to her, that's all. She made the right choice.'

There was something about that voice that made Jemima want to hit the boat's woodwork.

'You can't still be in love with her!' she cried from the heart.

'Can't I?'

Jemima wanted to die. It didn't show. 'I thought gamblers knew when to cut their losses.' Her voice was cool and hard as an ice sculpture. Here, you would say, was the Queen of Don't Care.

Niall shrugged. 'I guess I'm a one-woman man.'

Jemima was screaming silently with the pain. So why did she have to turn the knife in her own wound?

'Then maybe you'll go back and marry her one day?'

Niall did not answer.

She gave the stiletto another little turn. 'You might. What do you think?'

'Unlikely.' It was quite without emotion.

Another twist. 'Hey, don't give up. Maybe your luck will change.' She sounded positively bracing. 'Surely that's the upside about being a professional gambler? You could win enough to buy a mansion with swimming pool and helicopter. All the horses she wants. The full works.'

There was another, longer pause. Jemima had the sudden feeling that she was saying what Niall had said to himself a thousand times. And always answered the same way.

'But I'd still be me,' said Niall quietly.

CHAPTER SEVEN

THE day darkened after that. In every way.

Not that Jemima let her hurt show. She was, if anything, brighter than before. She lay down again, turning over so he couldn't see her too bright eyes, and encouraged him to apply the suncream. All the time she laughed and teased him, wittier than she had ever been in her life.

They ended by making shattering love again. Niall was passionate, attentive, absorbed. Everything that a woman could want. But when he fell asleep on her breast Jemima looked up at the clouds scudding in and wished she were anywhere else in the world.

Eventually she wriggled out from under him. Her clothes were still on the beach by the unlit bonfire, but she scrambled into the bikini bottoms, pulling a face at the sensation. She couldn't face the top—but he had to have a shirt she could borrow.

She found one in the little cabin. It was crumpled and it smelled of him. She shivered as she pulled it on. It felt like the enchanted beast in the fairytale—embracing her, engulfing her. The sooner she got her own clothes the better.

She slid over the side as quietly as she could manage.

The air had got heavy, somehow. In spite of the clouds it seemed hotter. The breeze was no longer fresh. To Jemima, perhaps over-sensitive, it seemed to smell of burnt-out fire. The sunlight was too bright, sharp like a circus spotlight. It hurt her eyes.

She thought, I must get away.

Suddenly it was like a physical craving. She could feel it all along her skin, in her bones, through her blood, where Niall had touched her. All the warning voices in the world

124

would not have stopped her. She *had* to get away from him, be alone, even for a little while. She had to find some way through this new anguish.

She turned her back on the beach, where she had laughed, the sea, where she had played, the boat where Niall Blackthorne had taken her to Paradise. Leaving her—where? She turned and fled.

She went round the little headland at a run. It was a mad scramble. Twice she had to put her hand down to keep her balance as she teetered her way over big boulders and pebbles as smooth as glass. The third time she nearly slipped into the sea that foamed about the rocks.

Careful!

She took hold of herself. The deck shoes he had bought her were not the greatest shoes for rock-climbing. She had to be sensible. She took the rest of the outcrop more slowly.

On the other side, she wandered along the new, pristine beach. Picking up a piece of driftwood, she swung it aimlessly. So—the man loved someone else. Really loved her. Didn't just fancy the pants off her.

Well, what did that matter to Jemima? She had only known him for—what? Thirty-six hours, tops. And most of that time she had been fighting him.

She should never have stopped fighting.

Come on, she told herself. You've got through worse than this. Basil made you ill and manipulated you until you couldn't think straight. You got back from that. You'll get through this too.

But Basil didn't break my heart.

She stopped dead.

Basil didn't break her heart? Did that mean that Niall Blackthorne could? Or even had?

Ridiculous.

But it didn't feel ridiculous. It felt horribly true. Jemima closed her eyes.

The bit of her that was trying to fight back took her to

task. Take it lightly, said Tough Jemima. You'll come through this.

Look at it this way: Oh, great, that's all I need—a collapsing career, a dedicated stalker and now a broken heart to go with it.

'Some holiday this has turned out to be,' she muttered. 'Oh, well, a change is as good as a rest.' Yes, that was better.

Behind her, a voice called her name sharply.

And now she had to put on the performance of her life!

She turned. Niall was balancing on the rocky outcrop. He was too far away for her to see his expression, but he looked concerned.

Straightening her shoulders, Jemima raised a hand. As if she were glad to see him. As if she were still glowing in the aftermath of that spectacular lovemaking.

He leaped lightly down and started to lope towards her.

Smile for the camera, Jemima adjured herself.

She pinned on a wide one and waited for him.

As he approached she tried to view him dispassionately. He had obviously failed to find his Bermudas. He was wearing ragged denim shorts, as he had been the first time she saw him. Criminal shorts, a pair of old canvas shoes with more holes than shoe, and a watch that an Admiral of the Fleet would have been proud of. And *nothing else*.

In spite of herself, Jemima's mouth dried.

He wasn't spectacularly muscular. Jemima had worked with plenty of male models and he wouldn't have given any one of them a run for their money. He was tall, but not overpoweringly so. He was tanned, but not burnt-toffee-brown. His hair was seal-dark and smooth, but nothing special by international model standards. And his odd, irregular face, with its bony nose and lazy hooded eyes, certainly wasn't handsome.

So why was he so devastating? Because he was. And she wasn't the only woman to recognise it.

Yes, that was the thing to hang onto. Jemima brooded.

She was one of many. It made her feel more of a fool, but at least it wasn't quite so frightening.

He reached her. 'You look very solemn.'

'Just thinking.'

'Is that all?'

He put an arm round her. She stiffened, then made herself relax. She had to get through a trip back to Pentecost without making a total twerp of herself.

She fell into step beside him, letting her head droop onto his shoulder. That way, she didn't have to look at him.

'Plenty to think about,' she said with determined gaiety. 'Have you seen the butterflies?'

They strolled along the rim of the beach, while Jemima pointed out brilliant butterflies that danced through the shrubs. Niall didn't know the names of any of them. He was sounder on the plant life.

'Acacia,' he said, flicking a savagely prickly bush. 'Thorns like daggers but smell that.' He snapped off a small branch and held it out to her. 'Smells of the sea, doesn't it?'

Jemima was startled. She recoiled instinctively. She did not want Niall the Heartbreak Pirate bringing her warm seductive scents to try.

'So it does,' she said without enthusiasm.

He stopped dead then, searching her face.

'What is it, sweetheart?'

The endearment made her eyes sting, even though she knew he did not mean it.

More likely *because* he didn't mean it, pointed out the Jemima who was fighting back.

She said, 'Nothing. Maybe I've had too much sun. It feels quite oppressive now, doesn't it?'

He looked at the sky. 'There's probably a storm coming. We should be probably go, if we want to outrun it.'

'Okay.'

'Or we could let it do its worst. Stay here overnight.' It was half a question.

Jemima said nothing.

He said softly, 'We could set light to that bonfire after all.'

It was so unexpected she gasped. It hurt like a knife-slash from nowhere. She knew she had been wounded to the heart, but the pain had not started. Yet it would come.

Niall's hands tightened on her arms. 'What *is* it, Jay Jay?' No sexy teasing now.

She swallowed, shaking her head. She could not speak.

He sighed. 'All right. We'll make a run for Pentecost. If you're sure that's what you want?'

'Absolutely.' Fighting Jemima took charge. 'I have just *got* to wash my hair. It's never felt so horrible in my life.'

It was even true.

He sighed and accepted it.

They went back to the first beach and gathered up their clothes. Niall stuffed everything into the bag with the undrunk beer. Jemima could hardly lift it. But he looped the strap over his shoulder and strode back to the boat as if it weighed no more than a piece of dried-out driftwood.

'You are so strong,' she teased. But it was an effort.

He smiled. But his eyes were questioning.

They stayed questioning all through the run back to Pentecost. But there was too much to do for him to demand any dangerous explanations. The sky darkened and the wind whipped even Jemima's sea-matted hair about her shoulders. By the time they sailed into harbour great fat drops of rain were splashing down onto the deck.

They ran for the big four-wheel drive. Not hand in hand this time. And though Jemima laughed, it was forced.

The rain had turned into a real howling storm. Niall concentrated on the road as a curtain of water drove across the windscreen.

He didn't take her to the lobby but stopped just below her block. He cut the engine and turned to her.

'Tell me, Jay Jay. What did I do?'

She edged away. 'Gave me a wonderful day,' she said lightly. 'Thank you. But my shampoo calls.'

She found the door handle and slid away before he could stop her.

Niall slammed on the brakes and stormed into the lobby before the car had stopped rocking. He went straight behind the reception desk where Al was sitting.

'Show me the ledger,' demanded Niall, spinning Al's chair round to face him.

'Can't. It's chuntering away to itself, updating. We've got another unexpected guest off the morning plane,' said Al, pleased.

'Congratulations. I thought you were playing solitaire to try and look busy.'

Al looked like a wounded bloodhound. 'You can be very hurtful.'

'Show me the ledger,' Niall said again curtly.

'Why?'

'Jay Jay Cooper. I want to see her registration again.'

Al protested, but Niall took no notice. He tipped him unceremoniously off the computer chair, sat down at the keyboard and tapped in the relevant information. He had sat in for Al often enough in the early days of Pirate's Point to know the system.

Yes, there it was. Credit card: Jemima Dare.

'Dare,' said Niall, frowning. 'Not Cooper. Now, why? She's married? Running away from her husband, maybe?'

'You mean she hasn't already poured it all out?' said Al cattily. He resented being turned out of his chair. 'You're losing your touch.'

Niall ignored him. Instead he clicked onto the internet and pulled up a search engine.

'What are you doing?'

'Finding out who I've just spent the day with,' Niall said savagely. 'Ah, here it is.'

And there she was. Jemima Dare. International model. In

a hundred provocative poses, she looked out of the screen as she had looked at him this afternoon. Wide, slightly tip-tilted eyes, with their hints of green and amber, meltingly unreadable. Again and again the diabolically kissable mouth was slightly parted. A pain twisted in his gut.

Al looked over his shoulder, irritation forgotten. He gave a low whistle.

'Whew. What a difference. She doesn't look like that now.'

Niall was furious. 'What are you talking about? She looks exactly like that. Siren.' It was not a compliment.

'"Gut-wrenching sensuality allied to Titania's ethereal provocation,"' he read aloud. 'Oh, yes, she's all that.'

'Coo,' said Al.

He did not know what to say. He patted his friend's shoulder in wordless sympathy. He was perfectly willing to get a good laugh out of Niall coming a cropper with one of his casual hotel flirtations. But this sounded serious.

'She's clammed up.' Niall was talking to himself. 'I shouldn't have fallen asleep. But—*why* won't she talk to me?'

Al shook his head. 'Women!' he said, kneading Niall's shoulder.

'I bet now she'll take off. She's obviously a bolter. If only—'

Al hoisted himself onto the desk and fixed his friend with a fishy eye.

'Niall, you're drivelling. Get real. She's a woman. You're you. She'll come round.'

Niall shook his head. 'Not unless I can get her to open up. She hasn't so far.'

'So have another go. What can I do?'

Niall looked at the screen. 'Not a thing. My bet is she'll be off tomorrow. And she'll avoid me like the plague to-night. And I don't know *why*.' He slammed his fist down on the desk, so close that Al flinched and nearly fell off. 'Nothing short of voodoo is going to help me now.'

'Voodoo, eh? I'll talk to Ellie,' said Al, passing the buck to a higher authority.

Niall got up and shot the chair into the back wall so hard that a potted plant lost several leaves and three files launched themselves off the bookshelf.

Al was impressed. 'I'll talk to Ellie *now.*'

Jemima spent so long in the shower her hands turned to prune skin and her face looked pink as a peeled blood orange. She put her hair through the full works—shampoo, condition, rinse, moisturise, gel, Velcro rollers. It took over an hour. It made her feel clean. It did nothing for the pain in her heart.

She was drying her hair when she heard the tap on the door. At once she thought, It's him!

She could hardly bear to open it and go back into full bright performance mode. But she couldn't bear not to.

She huddled the hotel's robe round her, tied a scarf over the rollered hair and braced herself.

'I'm very tired...' she began as she flung the door open, then, 'Oh,' flattened.

For it wasn't Niall. It was her hostess.

'Forgive me,' said Ellie, tripping into the room as if Jemima had invited her. 'But I wonder if I could ask you a favour?'

Since it wasn't Niall, Jemima didn't care who it was or what they wanted.

'Sure,' she said wearily. 'What is it?'

According to Ellie, one of the hotel guests had recognised her.

'She's right, isn't she? You're Jemima Dare the model? I've seen you in *Elegance.*'

'Then I won't try to deny it.'

'Well, you see, I wondered if you'd be our guest of honour at the party this evening? I mean, I know you're on a private holiday and everything, but by the time it gets into the papers you'll be long gone. And it could be a lifesaver for Pirate's Point.' Ellie clasped her hands. 'We put our life savings into this. And then everyone stopped flying. We're at about half capacity and that's as good as it gets. We'll be empty after Easter unless something happens.'

Jemima put a hand to her head. 'What a crazy world.'

'What?'

'You think if someone who is basically a substitute for a coat hanger stays here, it will make a difference to whether people want to come here for a holiday or not?'

Ellie was taken aback. The party was an instant invention to help Niall. The occupation figures, though, were real.

'Yes,' she said baldly.

Jemima puffed resignedly. 'Okay. I'm not doing much good at anything else. I might as well give your PR a boost. Though I warn you, if you want something dressy you're out of luck.'

Ellie could not believe her luck. She had not had much confidence in the PR party plan.

Now she said, 'No sweat. You can have anything of mine that will work. In fact, come and look now.'

That brought Jemima out of her zombie indifference.

'Oh, no. I can't go out like this. He—I mean people might see me.'

'Ah.' Ellie stored up that betraying syllable for future use. 'Not a problem. There's a sunhat on the balcony. Every room has a couple. Along with umbrellas,' she added with a grin.

Jemima bowed to the inevitable. 'Give me five minutes.'

She was in jeans and a shirt in two. Ellie's eyebrows rose. But she did not comment. Instead she whisked Jemima into one of the hotel's buggies and took her out to their private cottage.

'Who will come to this party?'

'Oh, all the guests who are around. The local tourism minister.' She did not say that he was her cousin. 'The editor of the *Queen's Town Messenger*. Maybe the local airline director.'

'Guests?' Jemima seemed to swallow something jagged. 'Niall?'

'Too right,' said Ellie, seizing the bull by the horns. 'The airline director has a massive crush on him.'

'Oh.' Presumably another woman who let him get away with murder, thought Jemima, trying hard to be amused.

Ellie led the way into a spacious pine-floored bedroom and flung open a walk-in closet.

'Take your pick. I've got everything from slit-to-the-thigh to the full Cinderella.'

Jemima had worn her fair share of slit-to-the-thigh on the catwalks of the world. She didn't want to parade like that in front of the Heartbreaker Pirate. He might think she wanted him to carry her off again. And if he did, she thought it would break her heart

'What's the full Cinderella?' she asked, with a very good assumption of lightness.

Ellie brought it out from the back of the cupboard. It was a loose muslin skirt, deeply frilled at the hem, and a draw-string top. It looked utterly plain, until you saw the exquisite embroidery, like a fall of leaves across one shoulder, mirrored in the skirt.

'Started out white, but everything goes to cream here if you let it dry in the sun,' said Ellie affectionately. 'I wear it with a scarf of sari silk or it looks a bit bridal.'

Jemima shuddered. 'I'll take the brightest scarf you've got,' she said firmly. The last thing she wanted was to go to a party decked out in sub-wedding finery if Niall Blackthorne was going to be there.

Ellie found her a scarf of worked emerald silk. It had little chips of glass on it that caught the light as she moved. It also, though Jemima tried hard to block out the fact, brought out the latent green in her wide brown eyes.

She took it back to her room. The party was at seven. She lay down on her bed and stared at the ceiling. The pain was beginning to bite now. Jemima lay there dry-eyed, almost welcoming it. It sure as hell put other things into perspective. All the fear and betrayal she had felt about Basil now seemed like very small beer.

At seven-fifteen she rolled off the bed, put on Ellie's pretty draperies, and sat herself in front of the mirror.

'This,' she told herself, 'is a professional engagement. Just do it.'

These days celebrity hairdressers vied to style her Titian hair. But there had been years when she did it herself. She took out the rollers and fluffed it out with rapid, expert movements. In a matter of minutes she had tumbled waves that gleamed like fire, like rubies set in gold, like wine.

Or so the editor of the *Queen's Town Messenger* would say once she had cornered him, she thought, her mouth quirking. She scribbled the phrases into her diary and shoved it back in her handbag.

Make-up wasn't so important as hair, but it still showed whether she was trying or not. And with Niall Blackthorne among those present she was going to put on the show of her life!

Her skin glowed pale gold from the day, so she did not add anything to it. She shaded her eyes very delicately with the merest hint of purply-grey. It would make them look wide, deep, and, she hoped, mysterious, but no one but an expert would be able to tell she had put any colour on her eyelids at all.

She painted her lips a defiant copper, using all the skill she had: pencil outline, lip-brush, talc over the first layer, lip-brush again, then ending with a gloss that was slightly darker on the lower lip only.

She glared at the mirror. If that didn't make him break out in a sweat, then she might as well go into retirement now, she thought with black humour. Though what she was going to do about it if her sexy mouth actually succeeded in bringing him crashing to his knees...

She stood up, waving an airy hand. 'Details. Details.'

She swept the glittering emerald scarf around her, fluffed out the luxuriant hair, and—

And marched out to show Niall Blackthorne that there were some women who could get along without him very nicely.

It was a beach party, Jemima found. She followed the burble of voices and the clink of glass along the terrace to a stone wall covered in headily scented angels' trumpets. The sound of conviviality led her on, along paths edged with plumbago bushes, their sky-blue blossom ghostly grey in the moonlight, and through a garden gate onto the beach.

Tall flambeaux had been driven into the sand. The party was happening in a pool of light that could have come straight out of a Rembrandt.

Jemima stopped. Swallowed. Braced herself. And stepped onto a small podium in front of the greatest concentration of light. Around her, the chat dwindled noticeably as people turned to stare.

As she had learned over the years, she did not acknowledge one of them. She stared over their heads, one hand on her hip in the classic pose. Then she tossed her hair and went into the sexy catwalk prowl that people expected. The conversation died to a back-of-the-hall muttering.

Jemima strode through the guests without looking to left or right, straight for the master of ceremonies.

'Hello, Al,' she said in a voice that was carefully calculated to carry. 'How lovely to ask me. A real Caribbean beach party!'

She air-kissed him, once on each cheek, careful not to smudge the work of art that was her mouth. The cameras started to click.

Al looked taken aback. 'You're gorgeous,' he blurted.

Jemima raised her eyebrows. 'Why, thank you.' She slid a hand through the crook of his arm and smiled at a photographer. 'Introduce me, darling.'

Al swallowed hard. But he walked her round the party in a bemused fashion.

The great and the good of Pentecost had clearly turned

out. Jemima said the right things about the island to the business-suited tourist minister and gave a couple of gossipy nothings to the editor in his Hawaiian shirt. It sent him off happy.

Then she talked clothes with the minister's wife—very New York, perfume with the director of the airline—very Paris, and Famous People I Have Met with just about everyone else, wearing anything from tuxedos to jeans. She talked and smiled and sipped at Planters' Punch without taking in a mouthful until her head was swimming and her feet ached.

And then the band started.

And Niall Blackthorne stepped out of the shadows.

Jemima's mouth dried. She took her first gulp of the rum cocktail.

'Dance,' he said.

'Are you asking me or telling me?' she said captiously.

He put an arm round her waist and walked her out of the light. 'Guess.'

'I can't dance with a glass in my hand.'

He took it away from her, tipped the drink unceremoniously onto the sand, and stuffed the sticky glass into the pocket of his jacket.

'Oh, very neat. You can always tell a misspent youth.'

'They trained us to think on our feet in the boy scouts,' he said gravely. But she knew he was laughing.

People were already dancing to the gentle, irresistible Caribbean rhythms. Niall took her into his arms and danced her backwards into the group. It was the lightest of holds. But Jemima could feel the heat of his hands through Ellie's silk and muslin.

The pain was suddenly almost suffocating.

He bent his head so that she alone could hear what he was saying. She could feel his breath stir her loosened hair. Crazily, she was glad that tonight it looked its gleaming best. For the first time he would see her as she really was. She might not match his *not impossible she*. But at least he would remember her.

He murmured in her ear, 'What are you running away from?'

Jemima was so startled that she stumbled. At once his hands tightened. The regret was suddenly so sharp that she caught her breath, unable to speak.

When it had passed a little she said, 'I don't know what you're talking about.'

'Don't you—Miss Jay Jay Cooper?'

She shrugged, though it was not easy to concentrate with his arms round her and his breath tickling her ear. 'I'm a celebrity. We travel incognito all the time.'

'Not so incognito that you have to pick up a bikini off a market stall,' Niall said shrewdly. 'Now, tell me the truth.'

'So I'm inefficient. It's not a crime.'

'And it's not celebrity behaviour either. And you're good at being a celebrity, aren't you?'

She gave him a blazing smile. 'I'm glad you noticed. I do my best.'

'So why did you turn up here with your hair in plaits and tell Al your name was Cooper?'

This was awful. Jemima closed her eyes briefly. 'I felt like it.'

'Nonsense.'

'Okay, I was tired of being a spoilt princess. I wanted to see what life was like for an ordinary backpacker,' she said desperately.

He laughed, but there was an edge to it. 'You'll have to do better than that.'

'I'm trying,' said Jemima between her teeth.

He was unsympathetic. 'Try harder.'

She made a sound that was pure frustration.

'I reckon it's got to be one of three reasons—career, money, a man. Which?'

'Not money,' said Jemima involuntarily.

'A man?' He looked at her searchingly. 'Husband?'

She shook her head.

'Boyfriend?'

'Please. Leave it alone.'

'A boyfriend,' he said, as if she had just confirmed it. 'What happened? You fell out of love? He did?'

'No. I could handle that,' Jemima said before she had time to think.

Niall's dark eyes sharpened. 'Sounds as if you could do with some help.'

Her laugh was pure despair.

'If you need a champion,' he said with precision, 'then I'm your man.'

No, you aren't. You're a one-woman man. And I'm not the woman.

Aloud she said coolly, 'I don't think so.'

Just as coolly, he said, 'Then you're wrong.'

Jemima drew herself up. 'What have my affairs got to do with you?' She was as frosty as she knew how.

'Let's say you intrigue me.'

'Gee, thanks.'

'And this afternoon we were lovers.'

It caught her unawares. Her whole body flinched.

Through a haze of pain she heard herself say brightly, 'Oh, that was just fun in the sun. You don't want to take it too seriously.'

His hands tightened alarmingly. 'You don't mean that.'

'This is the twenty-first century. Women have sex without the big production these days.'

'Some do.' He was grim. 'Not you.'

She was furious suddenly. 'Oh, you think you know me so well.'

'Are you saying I don't?' He was trying to sound amused, but the anger licked through.

'I'm saying you know nothing about me,' she flashed. 'Now, let me go. I don't want to dance with you. I never did.'

Niall's face went absolutely blank. His hands flew away from her as if she had stuck a pin in him. He stepped away from her with exaggerated courtesy.

She walked out of the light without a backward look.

She did not see the man who detached himself from the crowd and slipped after her. But Al did.

'Hey,' he said.

But the man had gone.

He looked round for his wife. 'Ellie,' he said urgently. 'One of the guests has just taken off after Jemima Dare.'

His wife was charming the Chair of the Chamber of Commerce. 'Lucky man,' she said.

'No, I mean she's gone off on her own along the beach. And he followed her. I don't think she knew he was there.'

Ellie knew an emergency when she saw one. She detached herself gracefully from the Chamber of Commerce.

'Along the beach? And you didn't stop him?'

'I called out. But he didn't hear me.'

'Or didn't want to.' She began to weave her way purposefully through the crowd. 'Who is he? Gambler or diver?'

'Neither. The character who arrived this morning off the Barbados plane.'

They looked at each other with deep foreboding. Ellie spoke for both of them. 'We need Niall.' She hopped up onto a wooden box and peered into the crowd. 'He's there.' She waved wildly. 'Niall, Niall. Over here. Quickly.'

Niall strolled over. 'Emergency? Do you want me to get some more beer?' The dark face looked as if he had been in prison for twenty years but he was making an effort.

What has she done to him? thought Al, indignant.

But Ellie had launched into an account of the stranger from the Barbados plane.

Niall's face changed, came alive. 'God damn it, he's a stalker. *That's* what she meant. Why the hell didn't she tell me? I'll wring her neck.' Then, to Al, 'Which direction did they take?'

'Away from the casino.'

To the loneliest part of the beach, in fact.

'Ouch,' said Ellie.

But Niall was already off and running.

CHAPTER EIGHT

THE breeze was full of the scents of the sea. The sky was like diamond-encrusted velvet. Jemima ignored both.

Try harder, indeed. Cynical bastard! She had been doing quite well, countering his questions, until he'd hit her with that.

'I'll give him *try harder,*' she muttered.

Did he think that he could strip her down to her darkest secrets? Did he think that one sexy afternoon entitled him to know everything there was to know about her? Just to keep himself amused?

Well, she wasn't playing. It was the devil's game.

I'm not available, my heart is given to a woman who won't have me—oh, but I'll take you on a little dance round the maypole, you lucky thing. Was that what he said to every woman? And they still came back for more? Honestly, sometimes she was ashamed of her own sex.

She ground her teeth audibly.

That was when she heard the sound of running feet behind her. Furious, she swept round, hands on hips.

'You sicken me,' she yelled. 'It's people like you who get men a bad name.'

She thought he would stop. Maybe yell right back at her. More likely give one of those infuriating superior laughs of his and tell her where she was getting it all wrong.

Only he didn't. Didn't yell. Didn't laugh. Didn't *stop!*

As the shadowy figure pounded down the beach towards her Jemima began to get a very bad feeling about it. The urge to scream at him died abruptly.

'Niall?' she said uncertainly.

In the moon shadows her pursuer could have been anyone. He was just a dark blur of greys moving steadily across the sand towards his target. There was something menacing in the way he had locked on to her and was just ploughing towards her, not fast, but somehow relentless.

'Niall?' she said again, hoping against hope. Knowing it wasn't.

He fetched up a few feet from her.

'Who's Niall? Your latest sucker?' said Basil Blane, panting.

Jemima drew a harsh breath. It was almost drowned by the rattle of the wind in the palm trees and the swish-swish of the tide at her back. But to her it sounded as loud as a scream.

To Basil too. He did laugh then. An ugly crowing laugh that made her skin crawl.

'What are you doing here?'

'"Whither thou goest…"' Basil swaggered forward. 'I told you I wouldn't let you go, babe. I found you. You're mine.'

The old familiar terror seemed to sweep round her like a cloak. It muffled all sounds but her own frantic breathing…his…

She said, bravely enough, 'I don't owe you anything.' But it seemed to die on the Caribbean breeze.

'Not true. And we both know that isn't true. You were a stick insect in a badly fitting uniform when you came to me.'

'I didn't come to you,' protested Jemima, temporarily stung out of her fear by the sheer injustice of it. 'You chased me.'

'I discovered you,' he corrected.

'I never asked to be discovered. You saw me in the school play and you wouldn't let go until my parents agreed to me doing those studio shots.'

'And you never looked back, did you?'

'Maybe I should have,' said Jemima slowly. 'I missed a lot of school because of you.'

'And you made a lot of money.'

She was silenced. She couldn't deny it. Her father had been made redundant. He hadn't complained, and he'd kept on looking for work, but everyone had known that he wouldn't find it. Not at his age. The bills had piled up; the mortgage had slipped. Then seventeen-year-old Jemima had started to earn session fees.

'Your family survived because of me,' he said intensely.

'I accept that everyone was grateful because I could earn some money—'

'Your damned sister wouldn't have finished college if I hadn't got you onto the teen circuit.' The anger flared out. 'And now she looks down her nose at me.'

That wasn't the whole truth and they both knew it.

Jemima began, 'You can't blame Izzy—'

He steamed straight over that. 'And you're worse. Now you've hit the big time you can't wait to get rid of me.'

'It's not like that.' Oh, God, she was doing the same thing as always: falling back on self-justification, as if he were in the right. Jemima heard the apologetic note in her voice. She hated it.

'Don't tell me what it's like.' Basil's voice was choked with rage. 'I *know* what it's like.'

He took a step forward. In the moonlight she could not make out his expression. But she could see that he was shaking.

'You used me. And now you think you can dump me?'

'I didn't!'

He wasn't listening. 'I did everything for you.'

'Altogether too much,' said Jemima dryly, though she was trembling

The lights of the party she had left were as far away as the moon. The sound of the steel band came and went on the breeze. She was all alone on the beach with a man who hated her.

Basil's hand flashed out. Jemima thought he was going to hit her and jerked away. But he caught her wrist instead.

She put her full weight into straining against his hold. But he didn't seem to notice.

'Oh, it's that again, is it?' he said grimly. 'Wicked Basil, trying to run little Jemima's life!'

She tried to stay calm. 'Let me go, Basil,' she said quietly.

He didn't even seem to hear. 'What the hell was I supposed to do? It was my job!'

'Basil, let me go and we'll talk.' She hated the pleading note in her voice. But she had never seen him like this before. She did not know what he might do.

He glared at her. His frustration, like a weapon, flourished in her face. 'You were my client. You *paid* me to run your life.'

He was clearly beyond reason. Jemima tugged her hands, but his grip was like iron.

'Only your bloody sister wasn't having it. She always hated me.'

His head was moving from side to side like a snake's. Suddenly she began to feel really afraid.

Jemima abandoned sweet reason. 'Stop it, Basil,' she said sharply.

It startled him enough to make him loosen his grip just a fraction. Jemima tugged her hands out of his and started to run. But she was wearing those wedge-heeled espadrilles again and she stumbled in the sand. She fell to one knee.

At once Basil was on her, grabbing and scrabbling, panting like a starving monkey. She felt Ellie's pretty dress twist to breaking point. Then tear. She fought back, but she was off balance and she had never hit anyone in her life. She did not succeed in doing much beyond protecting her face.

Basil was absolutely mindless. He tore at her as if she was a house he wanted to break into. And all the time he was muttering crazy things, phrases and half-sentences that made no sense.

Jemima tried to cry out. But she was so busy defending herself that she could not get enough breath or force her vocal chords into obedience. It was like the worst sort of nightmare.

'Mine,' Basil was saying again and again. 'Stupid. Ungrateful. Bitch. Mine. I'll show them. Mine.'

And then, amazingly, there were more footsteps, running towards them. Basil did not hear them. But Jemima did. With a great effort she heaved him off, scrabbled herself to her knees and cried out.

'Jay Jay?' called the voice.

Niall!

'Oh, thank God!' she exclaimed, half weeping.

Basil leaped back, snarling. This time he flung her onto the sand. She could smell the rum on his breath and the leather of his fashionable Italian jacket. He was pinning her flailing arms above her head, leaning heavily on her breasts. She thought he was going to suffocate her.

And suddenly she had the strength to fight back.

'Get off me,' she shouted, gasping for breath. 'You're vile. I hate you.'

'Jay Jay!' said the voice, a lot nearer. It sounded grim.

Basil was beyond noticing.

But Jemima wasn't locked in her voiceless nightmare any longer. She flung her head aside and yelled at the top of her lungs, even though her ribs felt as if they were on fire.

'Over here. Help. Help!'

The pain in her ribs stopped as if someone had taken the lid off a pressure cooker. She could feel the night air on her face again. She drew great gasping gulps of air into her lungs, eyes shut.

There were ugly sounds. Jemima struggled up onto her elbow, still breathing hard. A tangle of flying punches and wicked kicks writhed on the sand, grunting. She could not tell who was who—or who was winning.

'Niall,' she cried out, in quick alarm.

She hauled herself to her feet and looked around for a way to stop the fight. Her side hurt. She put a hand to it instinctively but it was not important. Somehow she had to stop the fight *now*, before someone got seriously hurt and it was all her fault.

Clearly there was no point in shouting at them. She looked round for a hose to douse them, a weapon to bring them to their senses. There was nothing. Not so much as a child's discarded bucket and spade. Not even a piece of driftwood.

And then she saw the little heap of darkness. Niall must have shrugged out of his dinner jacket before he plucked Basil off her. She picked it up. There was an ominous crackling and she thought—the glass! He put my glass in his pocket and it must have broken. Oh, well, it can't be helped.

She threw the jacket over the struggling pair. She tried to avoid their faces, though she wasn't sure whether she'd succeeded or not. The noises changed to frustrated rage.

Basil emerged first, spitting. But almost at once Niall was up too. He launched himself at Basil in a flying rugby tackle. It brought him down with a cruel thud. Niall crashed down on top of him, then consolidated his position with a knee in the small of Basil's back.

He looked up at Jemima. 'You're hurt.' His chest was heaving but he sounded totally in control.

She shot the hand away from her bruised ribs as if she had been burnt. 'No. I'm fine.'

'You don't sound fine,' said Niall, getting his breath back with startling rapidity. 'What did this piece of garbage do to you?'

'Nothing.'

'I saw him,' said Niall flatly.

She looked away. The lights of the party were bobbing about, smearing the fathomless sky. She blinked hard. It was no good. They were still more diffuse than they ought to have been.

And Niall was still waiting.

'Well, nothing major,' she muttered at last. She hoped— no, prayed—that the stupid tears didn't sound in her voice.

She couldn't bear it if he thought she was one of those drippy women who needed to be rescued all the time.

'Really?' He was politely incredulous. 'I don't think we agree on what is major, here.' His voice roughened. 'He had you on the ground.'

Basil stirred, muttering. Niall jabbed his knee and Basil subsided.

'Well?' he challenged Jemima.

She pushed her hair off her face. 'It's—complicated.'

'Complicated? Ah. So this is the not-boyfriend you couldn't handle.'

For some reason the hundred per cent accuracy of that infuriated her. 'Have you been taping our conversations?'

'I have a good memory.'

'For counting cards,' she said scornfully. 'Have you been counting my mistakes as well?'

Even in the shadows she could see his bafflement. 'What the hell are you talking about?'

Tears pricked her eyes. Reaction, she told herself. Aloud she said sharply, 'There's no need to shout at me.'

'I am not shouting,' he yelled.

Jemima looked away again. And this time there was no doubt. It was not just the shamefully girly tears in her eyes distorting her vision. One of the party lights was definitely bigger.

Not just bigger, moving.

'Someone's coming,' she hissed.

'Good. Then maybe we can get some sense here.' Niall looked over her shoulder and raised a hand in greeting. 'Hi, Al. What kept you?'

Al was carrying one of the flaming torches. It illumined a worried face before he lifted it high to survey the scene.

'Jay Jay, is that you? Are you okay?'

She nodded, suddenly terribly tired.

'It was real a stroke of luck that we saw that guy follow you,' said Al with feeling. 'What a relief for you.'

Niall was ironic. 'Not so's you'd notice.'

Basil had stopped struggling or even muttering. Niall removed his knee and stood up. A little stiffly, Jemima saw.

Her conscience smote her—rather late, admittedly. 'Did he hurt you?'

'What do you care?'

Al said hurriedly, 'Look, kids, let's continue the fight inside. I've got the island's great and good mingling back there. I don't want them thinking Pirate's Point is where you go for a fight on a Friday night. Be discreet, okay?'

Niall hauled Basil to his feet. 'How are you going to be discreet when Jemima charges this guy with assault?'

Al shifted from foot to foot. 'Can we talk about that indoors?'

Niall shrugged. But he applied a hand to Basil's collar and frogmarched him in Al's wake, pausing only to scoop up his jacket from the ground, where they had kicked it in their struggles.

Jemima followed wearily. She found that the borrowed blouse was sagging badly, leaving one shoulder bare. It skirted indecency by a whisker. Even in the shadows Niall would have seen the gleam of exposed flesh. It was almost the last straw. She held the front together convulsively, as if she could rewrite the last few minutes by sheer force of will.

Al took them to the terrace of his private cottage.

'Discreet, indeed,' said Niall dryly. 'But I warn you now—no cover-up. This thug—' he pushed Basil up the steps onto the decking '—could have injured Jemima seriously.'

In the light of the terrace lamp Basil looked pasty and rather sick. But he managed to pull himself together enough to say, 'You don't know what you're talking about.'

Niall looked at him with contempt. 'So explain it to me.'

Basil jerked his head at Jemima. 'Ask her,' he said sullenly.

Al seemed to think that was reasonable. But Niall's mouth thinned.

'I'm asking you,' he said with deceptive mildness.

Basil snorted. 'Got you hooked too, has she?'

Jemima sank into a rattan chair, wincing. Her ribs were really throbbing now, and she could feel a graze on the side of her face. Her naked shoulder was chilled under the breeze from the sea. She shivered.

Niall shook out his jacket and dropped it round her. Oh, hell, she must look really indecent, she thought.

'Thank you.' It was no more than a murmur.

He settled the coat about her shoulders, bunching her hair and pulling it over the collar. That made her wince too. He stepped away at once.

So much for her vainglory about her shining tresses this evening, she thought with irony. After her tussle on the beach, the lush waves were back to sand-filled tangles all over again.

Still, at least Niall was not looking at her now. Eyes narrowed to black slits of malevolence, all his attention was focused on Basil.

'Excuse me? ' he said softly

His tone chilled Jemima to the marrow. But Basil was not so alert to Niall's moods.

'Her,' he growled. 'The face of Belinda. God, I got that deal for her. And look what she did to me.'

'Basil, I—'

Niall ignored her. 'I'm looking at what you did to her,' he told Basil softly. 'And it tempts me to kick you all the way back down to the beach again.'

Basil sat down rather fast.

Al said hastily, 'Now, let's talk this through, Niall. We don't know the full story.'

Basil turned to him with eagerness. 'You are so right. This girl was nothing until I found her. I worked my guts out for her. Gave up all my other clients. And what did she do? Ditched me the moment she got the big contract.'

Jemima closed her eyes. It sounded so plausible.

'It's not true,' she said, knowing they would not believe her. Nobody who listened to Basil ever believed her.

Basil had been telling himself his version of the story for so long it was word-perfect. He believed it passionately. Even Jemima would have been convinced if she hadn't known the truth.

But she opened her eyes and made a last bid to tell the truth. Ignoring Al, she looked straight at Niall.

'I didn't ditch him. I would never have left him if—'

Basil interrupted, 'If her sister hadn't started working for their rich American cousin and decided I wasn't good enough for little sister any more.'

Jemima swallowed. This was the area she didn't like to look at too closely. 'It wasn't Izzy's fault.'

'You were happy with me until she started interfering.'

Jemima gave a shock of bitter laughter. 'And why did she interfere?'

'Because I wasn't smooth enough—'

Suddenly Jemima couldn't bear it any more. She surged to her feet. 'Because you were bloody killing me.'

The men blinked. Even Basil was momentarily shocked out of his sense of injury.

'You can't blame Izzy. It was nothing to do with Izzy. It was down to you and me, Basil,' she said with intensity. 'Just you and me.'

He began to bluster. 'That's crazy. We were fine until—'

'You might have been fine. I wasn't. When Izzy saw what you were doing to me she did what I should have done myself. That's all.'

Niall swung round, his eyes hot. 'What he did to you?'

Oh, God, she was going to have to tell him the truth. This was much worse than being shown up as a girly wimp. This was the big guns. He would really despise her after this.

'It's in the past. Over,' she said cravenly.

Niall strode over to her. 'Clearly it isn't.' His face was grim, but he touched her cheek with the gentlest of fingers. 'Your face is bleeding.'

'Oh, damn. Dirty hair and now a scab on my cheekbone,' she said, trying to make a joke of it. 'What will happen to my reputation?

But Niall wasn't to be deflected. She should have realised that once he'd got his teeth into her sorry past he wouldn't let go.

He was gentle. But utterly implacable. 'You'll always be gorgeous,' he said without expression. 'Enlighten me. What *exactly* did he do to you?'

'Yes,' chimed in Basil, triumphant. 'What did I do for you that you didn't want? Didn't beg me for?'

The look Niall turned on him was so malevolent that Basil actually shot back in his chair and put his hands up. 'Don't—' he said, frightened.

'Then don't interrupt the lady.'

Jemima pushed her hands through the ruin of her hair. Oh, well, get it over with, she told herself. Tell the truth. Don't look at Niall, so you won't have to see his reaction, then get out. And you won't have to think about it ever again.

In a voice as expressionless as his own, she said, 'Basil gave me pills. Appetite suppressants. Lots of them.'

'Oh, yes?' Basil was scornful. 'Did I hold you down and pour them down your throat?'

'No,' said Jemima painfully. 'You said I was getting so heavy that no one would use me. You said the camera showed every pound. You said that the fashion look was thin, thin, thin. I believed you. I wanted to do well. I chose to take the pills. You're right.'

'See?' Basil spread his hands, appealing to the others.

Niall was utterly intent. Jemima did not look at him. She could not bear to. But even so she could feel his eyes on her, like a magnet, dragging her into his force field.

Her breast seemed to burn with it. And, looking down, she saw that the damned blouse had slipped again. It was gaping and barely decent. In the circumstances, it was a small enough thing. But she could have cried.

Hurriedly, clumsily, she hauled the ruined material back over her bared shoulder and clutched it together, as if it could protect her from his scrutiny.

Niall made a wordless sound. Contempt? Anger? Disgust? She didn't want to know. She refused to look at him.

She went on in a low voice, 'He had me locked away in a London hotel. I was high as a kite and half crazy most of the time. My sister Izzy broke in and rescued me.'

There was almost total silence. Just the wind in the palms and the odd squawk of a nocturnal animal on a rummage in the undergrowth. Jemima looked across the handrail at the dark garden and the stars. She would never, she thought, ever forget those stars. They were all that stopped her seeing Niall's contempt.

How did she compare with his *not impossible she* now? A pretty shoddy substitute, that was all. And purely temporary. As she had always been.

She straightened her shoulders and told them the last, shameful, dangerous truth.

'She got me into a clinic. I spent a month detoxing.'

Utter, utter silence. Shock, presumably.

'When I got out, I told Basil I was leaving. That if he contested my contract I'd tell the courts what he'd done. I had the medical evidence after all. It would have finished my career, but—' she swallowed '—anything was better than going back to that.'

'I made you,' Basil blustered. But it was beginning to sound hollow. Perhaps even to himself, because he trailed into silence before anyone told him to.

'Since then he has stalked me. It's driven me half crazy. Dodging and weaving and making sure I always had the same chauffeur in case he hijacked my car and—' She broke off. 'Well, it's been horrible. I won't do it any more. No career is worth it.'

She walked past Niall without looking at him. She couldn't bear to look at him. She knew what she would see.

But she could feel the warmth of his body, like a familiar fire. She would have given anything in the world to be able to turn to that fire and feel it was where she belonged.

But she didn't deserve it. And she belonged with no one.

So instead she looked at Basil, who knew all the sordidness because he had caused it.

She said very quietly, 'This is the end, Basil. If you approach me again, I'll go to the police.'

'You wouldn't—' But she could see from the way his eyes shifted away from hers that he knew she would.

She shook her poor bruised head and managed not to wince. Well, that was something. A little dignity left, then.

'Like I said. No career is worth it.'

Her throat hurt. But she kept her head high. She turned to Al.

'I won't press charges this time. I owe him that. What you do is up to you.'

And then, to Niall, looking over his shoulder, she said in a voice as cool and remote as the moon, 'I hope you're not hurt. Thank you for your help tonight. It won't be needed again, I promise.'

She walked off the terrace and into the darkness of the garden before the tears spilled over and she made a terminal fool of herself.

It took her a while to find her way back to her own apartment. But there was no one waiting for her when she got there. So she was able to tip onto the bed and cry at last.

When she had finished crying, she got up, soaked her hot eyelids, washed her hair. Then, very carefully, she took the shards of glass out of the pocket of Niall's dinner jacket and wrapped them so that no cleaners could cut themselves on them.

And she took the dusty, sandy jacket, that smelled of the sea and his skin. And wrapped it round her.

Tomorrow she would leave, and she would go home and she would leave the jacket behind her. Maybe with a grateful note of thanks.

But for tonight, for the last time, with every sleeping breath she would inhale the smell of acacia and Caribbean night and woodsmoke that was uniquely Niall.

And that would have to last her.

CHAPTER NINE

THE next morning she was herself again, ultra-cool and ready for anything. Except for the grazed cheek and a slight blind look in her eyes when no one was looking, she was Jemima Dare, supermodel, in full working order.

She called the reception desk as soon as she got up.

'Will you make up my bill please? I'm leaving today.'

And the airline as soon as the office was open.

The staff were friendly but laid-back. There wasn't a connection to London available that day. She'd do better to stay over the weekend, they suggested cheerfully. She could go to the school sports day, the kite flying contest, give the local journalist a proper interview and generally chill out.

Jemima knew a small town strategy when she saw it.

'Put it this way,' she said sweetly, 'I'm getting off this island today. If necessary I'll hire a plane from Venezuela to pick me up. But I'm leaving.'

The airline clerk sighed. 'Well, it was worth a try. I can get you on the three o'clock flight to Antigua. Check in one hour before.' There was much tapping. 'You can get a connection there. First class, right?'

'Yes.'

'I've made the reservation. Hope to see you back soon.'

Not a snowball's chance in hell, thought Jemima. She was going to retire whichever bit of her subconscious the name Pentecost had floated out of.

'Thank you,' she said politely.

In theory, breakfast was over. But Pirate's Point had a relaxed attitude to things like mealtimes, she found. A couple of tables were still laid on the waterside terrace. The breakfast buffet had been cleared, but a smiling waitress appeared as if by magic to offer her all the bounty she could wish for.

'Coffee? Toast? The full English breakfast?'

Jemima shuddered. 'Just coffee, please.'

'Mango? Pineapple? Watermelon?' said a voice she knew.

She stiffened.

Niall strolled into view. He was back to ragged denim shorts and no shirt again. She wanted to touch his golden chest so badly her hands tingled.

Hands? Who was she kidding? Her whole damned body tingled. Everywhere he had touched yesterday remembered him. And he had touched pretty much everywhere. Jemima swallowed hard and hoped lust didn't show as unmistakably as it felt.

'Good morning,' she said in a suffocated voice.

'Hi.' He pulled out the chair opposite her. 'Bring a selection of fruit,' he told the waitress.

He sat down as the woman went off, grinning conspiratorially.

But Niall was not grinning. He searched her face for a long moment. Then, 'How are you feeling?'

Damn him, how could he look so concerned? As if she mattered to him?

Jemima's throat moved. 'Fine, thank you. A bit bruised.'

As he had done last night, he air-touched the graze on her cheekbone. 'That looks painful.'

She looked away, shrugging. 'What's more important, it looks ugly. I shall probably have to hit Harley Street on Monday morning. I've got a big shoot next week.'

He looked bemused. 'It hardly needs plastic surgery.'

She shrugged. 'Whatever it takes,' she said lightly.

Niall was briefly sidetracked. 'You're joking,' he said, appalled.

'Am I?'

She gave him a cynical smile. It was a good one, in the circumstances. You could hardly expect it to make it up as

far as her eyes. Not when every moment she looked at him
was filled with wild regret that he was a one-woman man
and she was not the woman. And never would be.

'God, you're in a crazy profession,' he said, from the
heart.

'You are so right,' she agreed cordially. 'But it takes me
round the world and gives me a lifestyle I could only have
dreamed about otherwise.'

He was grave. 'And that's important?'

'It keeps me out of mischief,' she said flippantly.

He reached out across the table and took her hand. 'But
it doesn't, does it?'

She couldn't bear the gentle teasing. She snatched her
hand away.

'It will in future. I've learned my lesson.'

'Jay Jay—' His use of the pet name was somehow the
last straw.

'Don't call me that!' she flashed. 'It's Jemima.'

He blinked. His eyes were so dark she could have
drowned in them. Damn it, she nearly had drowned in them.
Was it only yesterday?

'Okay, if that's what you want. Jemima—'

How could he be so not-handsome and so devastating at
the same time? None of the gorgeous men she had posed
with over the years had given her heart more than a passing
flutter. But Niall...!

You'll get over this. You have to get over this.

The waitress came back with Jemima's breakfast, and a
mug of fragrant coffee for Niall.

'Gordy from the *Messenger* called. He's on his way over
to see you,' she told them.

Jemima gave an elaborate sigh. 'He'll have to be quick.
I'm due at the airport at two.'

The waitress looked astonished. 'Nothing's quick on
Pentecost.'

Then how come I lost my heart in twenty-four hours?

Hell, not even that. Between one moment and the next.

Between falling asleep in his arms and waking to the smell of coffee. Between him kissing my grubby hair and me falling asleep.

Or maybe it was even sooner than that. Between his taking my hand on that beach, as lovers do, and us reaching the boat. Our boat.

Maybe that was it. One moment it was *mine* and *his*; the next it was *ours*. And she was in love. And it had taken a micro-second.

Jemima shivered. Oh, boy, she had got it bad!

Across the table Niall Blackthorne looked sexy and concerned and masterful. But he did not look like a man in love. Because he wasn't.

She had to snap out of it before she broke down and begged! She brought herself out of her reverie.

He was saying, 'But nothing is very far either. If he's leaving now, he'll get here from Queen's Town before this coffee is cold.'

Jemima managed another of her lower hemisphere smiles. 'Well, he can only photograph my best side.'

The waitress thought that was very funny. She went off back to the kitchen in gales of laughter.

Niall said gently, 'You really don't have to talk to him if you don't want to, you know. I can head him off at the pass for you.'

For a moment it felt like being loved. She savoured it, knowing she would hug it to her in the days to come.

Even so, she shook her head. 'No. It's all part of the job. My public wants a photograph. My public gets a photograph. That's the deal.'

His eyes were questioning. 'No private life at all?'

She gave him a bright smile. 'Not as long as I want to stay on top.'

'And do you?' He leaned forward. 'Want to stay on top, I mean?'

She looked away. 'It doesn't last, you know. I've got maybe a year. Maybe two. Then there'll be a new face, another hank of hair that the columnists rave about. And I'll be lucky to get one in ten of the jobs my agent pitches for. The world is full of women the world once called top models who are lucky to get an elastic stocking ad.'

He laughed. 'That's the fate that awaits you?'

'Almost certainly,' she said gaily.

'Live fast and hard and the devil take tomorrow?' he suggested.

Her heart hurt. 'Got it in one.' Oh, she sounded so indifferent, so careless! Well done, Jemima!

His eyes were grave. 'So there wouldn't be any point in a man asking you to wait for him?'

What was he talking about? He didn't want her to wait for him. He didn't want her at all. If he did want her she wouldn't have to wait, after all. It wasn't as if you had a three-month contract with the gambling tables.

'Not a chance.' Her voice was brittle.

Niall was silent.

'Grab it now. Nothing lasts. That's my motto.'

He looked at her broodingly. 'You really mean that?'

'Consider yesterday,' she said, though the pain was so great it was almost physical. 'Did I seem to you like a put-it-off-till-tomorrow kind of girl? If there's a new sensual experience on offer, get your hands on it now.'

Niall's mouth twitched unexpectedly. 'Well, it was certainly sensual,' he said dryly. 'Remarkably so.' He beamed at her, but she sensed something real underneath it. 'Memorable.'

It was so unexpected Jemima gasped. She felt the colour sweep up her bruised face like a tidal wave in a horrifying tide.

'Damn!' she said, nearly in tears all of a sudden and hating him for it.

He did not pretend not to notice. 'Blow your nose and have some fresh mango,' he said unsympathetically. 'That's another great sensual experience you shouldn't put off.' His voice bit.

Jemima realised suddenly that she couldn't take any more of this.

'I'm not hungry,' she choked. And fled before he could stop her.

She shot back to her room. The tears had subsided by the time she got there but it had been a nasty feeling. She packed with shaking hands.

She came across the day-glo bikini he had bought her and her heart lurched.

But— 'No mementoes,' she said firmly. 'You'll get over him, but not if you keep a bunch of keepsakes. Time to get real.'

She stuffed it in the wastepaper basket and zipped up her flight bag. It seemed tiny. So little luggage, so little time— and her whole world had turned upside down.

Still, look on the bright side. At least you've finally dealt with Basil, she told herself. You're not afraid of him any more. Or anyone.

It was true. Heartbroken? Maybe. Afraid? Nah. Never again.

She had the chance to prove that almost at once. When she went to the lobby to pay her bill Niall was there, his back to her, talking to Al. She hung back, gathering her forces.

'...second chance,' Al was saying.

Niall was impatient. 'Not this time.'

'Hey, marriages end.'

Niall laughed reluctantly. 'You're a happily married man!'

'Sure. And I've been at the luxury end of the tourist trade all my life,' said Al cynically. 'Half our wedding trade is people who need to get away from the congregation who witnessed their last fling into matrimony.' He was riffling through papers. 'Your lady may come back onto the market yet. Don't give up hope.'

He was talking about That Woman again. The one who wanted the cats and dogs and horses and broke his heart to get them! Jemima found that her fingers were curling into claws and hurriedly straightened them.

It was nothing to do with her, she reminded herself. Niall Blackthorne made his own choices. She didn't even figure in his calculations. But why couldn't he wake up and move on? It was such a waste!

And not a thing she could do about it. After all, she could hardly say, Cut your losses and settle for me, could she? Not to a one-woman man who had cherished his hopeless love for years.

Anyway, she didn't want him to cut his losses. She didn't want to be second best. She wanted him to realise that there could be a second woman and it would be glorious. She wanted him to fall in love with her.

Fat chance. He had already told her as much. He thought she was money-grubbing trash in a hurry. And he thought it because she had told him so.

I must be out of my mind, thought Jemima, astonished at her own behaviour. The sooner I get out of this hothouse the better.

She strode up to them, chin high.

'Hello.'

They both turned. Al smiled, but Niall's face was unreadable.

'Bill, please. And can I order a taxi to take me to the airport?'

'I'll drive you,' said unreadable, tanned, shirtless Niall.

Oh, it wasn't *fair*.

'I wouldn't want to trouble you.' Her tone had an edge to it.

'Tough.' So had his. 'You do trouble me. You have from the start. It's never worried you before.'

Al looked from one to the other, open-mouthed.

Jemima glared. 'All the more reason not to see any more of each other.'

'I'll drive you,' said Niall obstinately.

'I won't go with you.' She was thoroughly roused.

'Oh, won't you?'

'Hey,' said Al, making the sort of gesture a conductor used to reduce the orchestra's volume. 'Keep it nice, kids. Jemima, the cabs are all meeting a cruise ship today. But if you really can't bear Niall's company any more, you can hitch a lift back into town with Gordy.'

'Sure,' Niall said savagely. 'Good idea. Get some more free publicity while you're at it.'

Jemima stuck her nose in the air. 'I hardly think I need it. Why do you think he's coming out here in the first place?'

He laughed angrily.

But she was wrong. When the editor arrived, he did not so much as look at her.

He walked past her, past Al, past the potted palm. Went straight up to Niall and took off his dark glasses, smiling.

'Niall, man. Good to see you.'

Niall's eyes narrowed. 'Hi, Gordy. You saw me last night.'

'And this morning I got a nice e-mail with a photo attachment.' Gordy put a hand on Niall's shoulder and grinned from ear to ear. 'You are the Duke of Powrie and I claim my prize.'

Niall gave a roar.

Shock? Fury? Dismay? All of those, thought Jemima. But not denial. He was the Duke of Powrie all right.

That was when she had her moment of revelation. *He was an aristocrat*. She should have realised when he'd said that he was the spare of 'the heir and the spare'. That was why he didn't blame his *not impossible she* for her list of absolute essentials. Jemima thought they were shallow and the woman sounded like a gold-digger. But Jemima was not from that world. And Niall was!

Looking across the lobby, she had the oddest sensation that there was a galaxy of distance opening between them. More than a galaxy. A universe. He had not moved, but he

seemed as if he was so far away that if she called his name
he would not be able to hear her.

She stepped back, and back again. Nobody noticed. She
retreated further, faster. Gordy and Niall were still arguing
heatedly, with Al acting as referee. It was the ideal opportunity. She left.

She found Ellie in the kitchen.

'I need to get out,' she said baldly. 'I've saved face until
my teeth ache and I'm all out of good behaviour. Help!'

Ellie stopped giving her kitchen staff instructions and
looked at Jemima shrewdly.

'Niall?'

Jemima shook her head. 'Don't ask.'

Female solidarity kicked in. Ellie took the credit card
away and processed payment for the bill that Al still had
not managed to prepare. Then she handed over the kitchen
to a trusted aide, got out the family runabout, and took
Jemima to the airport.

'What shall I tell him if he wants to get in touch?'

'He won't.'

'But if he does?'

'I hope he has a nice life.'

Jemima never afterwards remembered the flight back. She
might have been at risk of some really bad PR. If an am-
bitious paparazzo had got a shot of her with her hair mussed,
her cheek swollen and grazed and her eyes red he could
have sold it for thousands. It wouldn't have looked good at
all.

But nobody recognised her. Or if they'd thought they had,
she thought afterwards, they hadn't believed their eyes.

She went straight to the flat. This time she was glad it
was empty. She couldn't face Pepper or Izzy. They were
her family. More, they were her friends. But they were in
love and they thought love was a happy thing. Whereas she
knew it was a hungry, sleepless wild animal that gnawed
and gnawed at you. And the only thing worse than being

gnawed was when for a moment it stopped and you were afraid that you were forgetting.

I must be mad, she told herself.

But it sure as hell put other problems in perspective.

Her manager at the model agency took one look at her puffy cheek and freaked.

'Get a life,' said Jemima wearily.

She got a shot to reduce the puffiness and then went off to her favourite make-up artist to camouflage the remaining injury. And when she got to the shoot she found the photographer, whom she had always regarded as a bit of a pill, took it as a challenge.

He kept to her good side mostly. But then he took some sultry shots of her peering out from under a Philip Marlowe hat-brim. They both giggled a lot. Then they went out to dinner, where a paparazzo caught them with their arms round each other, laughing helplessly.

If Niall saw that, thought Jemima, he would know she was over him.

Madame got in touch again. But this time Jemima obeyed the summons to the House of Belinda in an entirely different spirit.

She strode into the luxurious office and said, 'Cards on the table,' before Madame had got halfway across the room to meet her.

'I'll do my job. I'll be Belinda's ambassador. I'll do the parties and the premieres and the interviews. But I'm not dating anyone because you think he will look good on my CV. If that's what you want, we can tear up the contract now.'

Madame's thin black eyebrows hit her hairline. But all she said was, 'Very well.' And designed a new campaign: *The Face of Belinda—Her Own Woman.*

'My life,' announced Jemima to her sister and cousin, 'is well and truly sorted.'

* * *

Niall got back to London at last in June, in a bleakly un-
seasonable rainstorm.

He walked out onto the main concourse of Terminal 4
with his suit-bag over his shoulder and all his other posses-
sions in a battered squash bag. Passport Control ignored
him.

Good, thought Niall. But he wondered how long it would
last. Did you have to have Duke of Something on your
passport? Oh, well, he would find out soon enough.

It had been a bumpy flight. Hardly anyone had slept. But
all around him people who could hardly stand for weariness
were putting on a spurt to run into someone's arms.

Niall was not exhausted. But there was no one for him
to hug. .

Well, that was good too. He had never wanted people
meeting him, laying claim to him, relying on him. He had
always taken good care to keep his life as he liked it—
unencumbered. And the only thing he had ever had in common with his father was a hatred of public emotion.

So it was a nasty shock to discover that if Jemima Dare
had been here to greet him, he would have dropped the bag,
flung his arms wide, swung her into them and kissed her
immoderately.

And then taken her off to the nearest hotel room and made
love to her until neither of them could move. If they'd managed to make it as far as a hotel!

Niall swallowed, suddenly hot. He ran a finger round the
inside of his collar. The bad flight must have had more of
an effect than he'd thought.

He wove his way through the hugging, kissing, weeping
crowd and told himself how grateful he was that he was
alone. Alone was what he liked best. Alone kept him strong.

There was no point in looking for Jemima. She did not
know he was coming. Nobody, not even the estate's lawyer,
who had been writing to him in tones of increasing desperation, knew he would be on this flight this morning. Besides,

even if she had known she would not have come to meet him. She hated him. She had not even said goodbye.

Of course he had not accepted that. Niall, who had never had to pursue a woman in his life, had mounted an impressive campaign. He had called, e-mailed written. Sent flowers. Even a mango.

None of it had got a whisper of reply. You would think she had vanished from the face of the earth.

Except for the gossip columns, of course. As he had kept his cool through the last dangerous weeks of his present assignment he had seen plenty of those. The net kept him well up to speed with the doings of Jemima Dare. She was dating a photographer; having a rose named after her at the Chelsea Flower Show; dancing all night at a charity fundraiser.

Niall damned all fundraisers and flowers, and double-damned photographers.

A man in a grey chauffeur's uniform was standing by the barrier with a large piece of card. 'Passenger Blackthorne', it said.

Niall stopped dead. But nobody knew he was coming, surely?

He went over to the man. 'Blackthorne?' he said, still thinking that there must be another Blackthorne on one of the flights coming in, from Addis Ababa or Tokyo or Banjul...

The neat man dispelled the hope. 'Good morning, Your Grace. Welcome home. I have the limousine outside. May I take your luggage?'

Not being met by Jemima was one thing. Being tracked down by a man with a limousine was unbearable. This was what it was to be a duke. His life would never be his own again.

There were more Your Graces at the discreetly exclusive hotel in St James's, where his lawyer had reserved him a room. A butler masquerading as a desk clerk welcomed him, congratulated him on his accession to the title, and asked about enquiries from the press.

'Enquiries?' said Niall, puzzled.

'We have had several telephone calls from people asking whether you are staying with us, Your Grace.'

'From journalists?'

The butler permitted himself a small smile. 'Such people do not normally identify themselves, Your Grace. We have learned to read the signs.'

'Wow,' said Niall, genuinely impressed. 'You must give me a few tips.'

The butler bowed. 'We shall be happy to, Your Grace.'

Niall groaned. 'Every time someone says Your Grace, I look behind me expecting to see my father. And now I suppose I'll have to put up with it for the rest of my life.'

The butler drew himself up to his full height. 'In this hotel, sir, we will call you whatever you wish.'

'How about Mr Blackthorne?' said Niall, amused.

'The staff will be informed.'

He was as good as his word. When Dom Templeton-Burke came round for a drink a couple of days later, the staff at the desk robustly denied that the Duke of Powrie was staying with them.

'But there he is,' said Dom, catching sight of Niall coming down the main staircase. And when a quiet porter politely barred his way, he said, 'He's my cousin, for heaven's sake. He asked me.'

The porter would still not have let him pass, but at that moment Niall caught sight of him and came over.

'You're early,' he said. 'I was just going to tell the desk I was expecting you. They're very—er—protective.'

'They're good,' said Dom. 'They were all set to throw me out.'

Niall grinned. 'That's my friend Jeeves.'

'What?'

Niall led the way into the bar and summoned the barman. 'Jeeves. He's supposed to be the desk clerk. But he's actually something between a life counsellor and a Mr Fixit. If you're a guest here, apparently, you can have anything you want.'

'Great,' said Dom enthusiastically. 'I could do with a new design of snowshoe.'

'He'll probably find it,' said Niall. 'He's turned me into a non-duke, God bless the man. Within these walls I'm plain Mr Blackthorne again.'

Niall had been at school with the Templeton-Burke brothers, and spent long parts of the holidays with them. Dom had a very fair idea of what life been like in the Powrie household.

'Getting to you, is it?' said Dom with rough sympathy.

They ordered their drinks, and while they were coming Niall said, 'You have no idea what a relief it is to talk to someone who doesn't think I should be out partying every night with delight.'

Dom raised his eyebrows.

'I think I probably hated my father,' Niall said reflectively. 'All these years I haven't really thought about him much. But I realised the other day, when I was looking at the mess that he and Derek between them have made of the estate. And I thought, they were pigs, both of them. Idle, spendthrift, stupid pigs. And malicious, too.'

Dom was startled. It showed.

'Oh, yes,' said Niall. 'My father stopped me going to university to read maths, just because he *could*. Pure spite. And Derek thought it was cool to be like him. Nothing has been repaired on the estate for three years. All the money went on Derek's pathetic racing cars. It's going to be absolutely bloody turning it around.'

'But you will?' said Dom.

'Yes, I will.'

'What you need,' said Dom, 'is a nice wife to help you. Get Abby to break out the gumboots and pearls brigade. Find yourself a woman who knows her Chippendale and her slurry pits, and you're laughing.'

Niall smiled but his tone was final. 'I think not.'

Cheery Dom realised that he was on delicate ground. 'Oh. Sorry. There's a lady in the case, is there?'

Niall shrugged. 'Maybe.'

'Well, come on, Niall. Either there is or there isn't.'

'Well, there is,' admitted Niall. 'Only she isn't talking to me.'

Dom's eyes sparkled. 'Terrific. Carry her off at midnight.'

'You,' said Niall resignedly, 'don't change. Grow up.'

'That's fine, coming from a man who's spent the last fifteen years gambling his way round the world,' retorted Dom. But his indignation was short-lived. 'Come on. I'll help you. Who is she?'

But Niall shook his head and refused to be drawn.

'My sort-of cousin is in a bad way,' confided Dom to his beloved as they cuddled up on the sofa watching a film that night. 'He's living in a hotel under an assumed name. I think he could do with some home comforts. Could we throw him a party?'

'Sure,' said kind Izzy. 'Your sort-of cousin is my sort-of cousin.'

Dom hugged her. 'Did I ever tell you what a wonderful woman you are?'

'Frequently, but keep it coming. What's wrong with our sort-of cousin?'

Dom pulled a face. 'He's a duke and he doesn't want to be.'

Izzy choked. 'We'll help him forget,' she promised.

So that weekend Niall found himself invited to a party to meet his new cousin-to-be.

'I'm Niall—friend of Dom's.'

'You got here. Great,' said the large redhead who opened the door.

'Well, Dom's instructions were a bit polar: turn north, leaving Arcturus on your right,' said Niall dryly. 'But he's told me how to get to places before, so I bought an *A to Z*. And London hasn't changed that much since—'

He stopped dead. A glamorous redhead in silky trousers and not very much top had emerged. His mouth fell open.

'You think you've met her before,' said Dom, following the redhead. He slapped a glass of wine into Niall's hand. 'Niall, Izzy. Izzy, Niall.'

'Hello,' said Niall faintly.

'Optical illusion, mate. Happens all the time. You haven't. But you've seen lots of photographs of her sister. Jemima is a model. Got her picture everywhere.'

Niall recovered. 'I've seen a lot more of Jemima than a photograph,' he said with feeling.

Which was unfortunate. Because that was the moment at which Jemima came out of the kitchen.

She seemed to freeze to the spot.

'Jay Jay?' said her sister, puzzled. Then, in concern, 'Jay Jay, are you all right?'

Niall could not take his eyes off her. She was carrying a tray of champagne flutes and she was laughing. Or she had been laughing before she saw who he was.

Her hair was loose, a wonderful fiery, silky mass. It had haunted his dreams and brought him out in a cold sweat in the middle of business meetings if he didn't keep an iron grip on his thoughts.

She was wearing a brief boned top in shiny emerald satin and dark green jeans. Her shoulders were bare, but this time not because some thug had attacked her. The pale exposed flesh did not make her look vulnerable. It made her look gorgeous and sexy and all too accessible.

Accessible! And she hadn't returned a single one of his calls!

He said glacially, 'Hi, Jemima. Remember me?'

The wonderful brown eyes flashed. 'Oh wow, the Duke! How could I forget?'

Dom groaned. Even Izzy looked slightly shocked.

Jemima put her tray of glasses down carefully.

'Not that he told me he was a duke,' she said, smiling nastily. 'I wonder why?'

'I haven't been a duke all that long,' said Niall, taken aback. 'And I had a job to finish before I started a new life.'

'A job?' Jemima gave a light, tinkling laugh that brought Izzy's brows together in a sudden frown. 'Gambling?'

Niall met her angry glare head-on. 'It's inferior to being a glorified coat hanger; I can see that,' he agreed amiably. 'But in this case I was gathering information for someone else.'

Jemima appeared surprised. 'Is that legal?'

The others came out of their shock. 'Come on, you probably remember Philip from school. He's just got back from China,' said Dom, linking his arm hurriedly with Niall's and urging him towards the other room.

'I couldn't find anything to put the pistachio shells in,' said Izzy. 'Can you help me, Jay Jay?'

So they dragged them apart like playground combatants, thought Niall. He let himself be delivered to Philip from China without a fight.

He was shaken. In desperation, he had begun to pull ducal strings to contrive a meeting with Jemima. And here it was, offered to him on a plate. And she hated him.

They circled each other like enemies throughout the party. But eventually, as people were beginning to leave, he cornered her in the cramped hallway.

'Jay Jay—'

Quick as a snake, she said, 'Don't ever call me that. What are you doing here?'

'I'm in the UK full-time now.'

She tittered. 'Lucky UK. But I don't care about your travel arrangements. What are you doing in *my house*?'

'I thought it was Izzy's house,' he pointed out. He thought she flinched, but she recovered so fast she couldn't be sure.

'Oh, yes, you're the hopeless not-quite cousin,' said Jemima. Niall could see she was working herself up to be as nasty as she could. 'I wondered what was wrong with the mystery man. I suppose being a duke of no fixed abode is getting you down?'

'I have several fixed abodes,' said Niall, stung. 'A tumbledown castle in Scotland and leases on several flats that my father and brother took for their own dubious purposes.'

'And you're living in a hotel?'

'While I work out what to do next.' He decided this nastiness was actually quite encouraging. 'You're very interested in my living arrangements.'

She flushed bright red. 'I don't give a damn where you live. As long as you don't try to worm your way into my life.'

'*Worm my way?*' He was outraged. 'You're out of your mind.'

'Oh, am I? Do you really expect me to believe that you came here tonight just because Dom took pity on you?' The words bit.

He looked at her very straightly. 'Why wouldn't you believe it? When have I ever lied to you?'

'Not in so many words, maybe. But you didn't tell me you were a duke, did you?'

The beautiful sensual mouth was trembling. Niall was furious with her. But he also wanted to kiss that tremulous mouth until she stopped hitting out and listened to the truth.

He said, with all the calm at his command, 'And you didn't tell me that you were running away from a stalker. That makes us even, I'd say.'

Calm didn't work. Flames shot out of Jemima's eyes.

'I didn't tell *anyone* about Basil,' she shouted.

Niall froze at that. Suddenly, calm was not an effort. His brain worked at the speed of light.

He said quietly, 'You didn't tell them? Not anyone? Not even your sister?'

She shrugged, not answering. But her breath was coming fast and there was a tiny pulse hammering frantically at the base of her throat. She wanted him to think she was angry, but there was a lot more than that going on here. Oh, God, he wanted to take her away and—

He stopped himself. *Patience, Niall. Patience.*

'And have you told them now?' he said in a still voice.

The flames subsided. Jemima's eyes slid away from his. 'What's to tell?'

He snorted disbelievingly. 'So I'm the only one who knows that Basil hounded you halfway round the world? Oh, that's just great.'

She was instantly defensive. 'Why should it matter to you?'

'It matters,' said Niall deliberately, 'because for a day you were mine.'

She gave a sort of gulp, as if she had fallen into a swimming pool and was drowning.

That was when he lost his cool completely.

'And should be again,' he said savagely.

He had never kissed anyone like this—harsh and desperate. When he let her go her eyes were wide with shock and she was shivering. All the sweet responsiveness of that day on the boat might have been a fantasy of his own imagination.

He stepped away from her.

'I'm sorry,' said Niall. He felt chilled to the bone, like marble. 'I shouldn't have come. I won't again.'

CHAPTER TEN

JEMIMA got along just fine on her own until Pepper's wedding.

Even that should have been okay. Between them Izzy and Jemima had talked her out of her worst excesses in the matter of bridesmaids' dresses. In the end, one of the young designers who worked for *Out of the Attic* came up with a shimmering bronze gown for Pepper and put the bridesmaids in simple dresses from the same bit of the spectrum— dark honey for Izzy, summer peach for Steven's delighted ward, greeny-gold for Jemima.

'It will be lovely,' he assured them. 'All that red hair and sunshine colours. You'll be spectacular.'

Pepper looked nervous. She had already vetoed a white wedding dress on the grounds that it would make her look like a sheet on somebody washing line, bulging with wind.

'I don't want be spectacular. Clean and tidy will do just fine,' she said.

But the sisters laughed her into submission.

And then Izzy suddenly got worried that Jemima would walk into the party afterwards alone.

'Do you want to bring someone? That new photographer of yours, maybe?'

'No, thanks.'

'Oh, but why? I'm sure Pepper would love to have him there.'

'Maybe she would. I can do without him.'

Izzy searched her sister's face. She was very serious suddenly.

'Are you sure? I mean, it must get you down—Pepper

173

and me flitting about with twigs in our beaks, nest-building all the time.'

'It's pretty tough to take,' Jemima agreed dryly. 'But I can handle it.'

'And it really wouldn't be fun to have a guy of your own to take you to the wedding?'

Oh, Niall, Niall.

'It really wouldn't be fun,' Jemima confirmed steadily.

Izzy said slowly, 'You're different.'

Jemima was flippant. 'I'm out from under your apron strings. It had to happen some time.'

'It's not that. When Basil Blane messed you up like that, I thought you came back brilliantly. But it seemed as if you were watching yourself all the time, in case you slipped over the edge again. Now—I don't know—it's as if you've stopped worrying, somehow.'

'Got my bottle back,' said Jemima lightly.

But Izzy didn't laugh. 'Yes, I think maybe you have.'

'Good.'

Izzy hadn't finished, though. 'That isn't why you don't want to bring Phil the photographer to the wedding, though, is it, Jay Jay? In case he's another Basil?'

Jemima put her hands down on the table—they were in the kitchen, surrounded by files and wedding lists—and stood up.

'Listen,' she said quietly. 'I don't give a flying fig about Basil. And I'm not afraid of men. I *am* afraid of pretending.'

Izzy frowned, puzzled.

'You're in love, right?' said Jemima.

Izzy nodded enthusiastically, her face breaking into a smile as it always did whenever she thought of her Dom.

'Well, I'm not. And I don't want a man on my arm like some sort of jungle camouflage. If I'm in love—' She corrected herself. 'If I fall in love with someone who loves me, sure, fine—I'll show him off proudly. If I'm not—well, I'm just as proud to be on my own. Being in love is too important to play games with.'

'You *have* changed,' said Izzy slowly. 'When did you get to learn so much about being in love?'

When I met a one-woman man.

Jemima shrugged, not answering aloud.

'Maybe you've found someone?' said Izzy, unusually hesitant.

Jemima sat down again and gathered Pepper's lists about her. 'And maybe I was born to be alone. Either way, I'll survive.'

The day of wedding dawned, as all the best weddings should, bright and clear. It was taking place in the chapel at Steven's Oxford college. So the photos—and the party, if the weather was kind—were scheduled for the Master's Garden.

Jemima got through the ceremony pretty well. She managed to look misty-eyed when Pepper promised to have and to hold, instead of screaming in pain, which was what she wanted to do. She prevented an enterprising pageboy from standing on Pepper's train. And by sheer force of personality she made Windflower—'call me *Janice*'—give the bride's flowers back after the couple signed the register.

She sat for some lovely photos with the other honey and gold bridesmaids. She did some dreamy shots in a cloud of roses on her own. She did not flinch when Izzy unselfconsciously reached up to her Dom and said, 'Our turn next, lover.'

So she was doing fine. And then—

She had been a bit surprised when Pepper wanted to ask Abby Diz. Sure, the woman had worked on the *Out of the Attic* account. But they were hardly close friends. In fact Jemima saw more of her than Pepper did.

But Steven had an enormous guest list—family, old friends, mates from the business he had built up from nothing, colleagues from the college. Pepper needed to boost her side of the chapel, she said. And Abby was going to be Izzy's sister-in-law. She was nearly family.

So Abby came, with her dashing, adoring Argentine husband. And a very distinct bump.

Not even that would have mattered, if only…if only….

Jemima left the amateur photographers in the rose garden and walked back towards the party and saw—

And saw Niall Blackthorne, almost unrecognisable in grey morning clothes and a pearly cravat, talking to the gorgeous Lady Abigail.

A heartbreaking ghost whispered her ear, *'Not my Abigail.'* And she remembered where she had first heard about the island of Pentecost.

'Where's that?' she had said. 'South Seas?'

And Abby—*Abby*—had shaken her head and said, 'Who knows? Could be. He gets around.'

Jemima felt as if someone had poured ice down her gold silk back. Suddenly her legs were trembling. She sank down onto a wooden bench, gift of a former master's wife, and tried to get her head round it.

'He's known me since I had spots and braces on my teeth,' Abby had said.

Why hadn't she remembered? Why? She'd had all the clues. She had even asked Abby if her husband should be worried.

'Stupid. I've been so stupid.'

But she was not the only one, Jemima realised. Because Abby had said something else too, secure and blind in her love for her husband. 'If there's one man in the world for whom I have no mystery, it's him.'

How wrong she was. Mystery? She had his whole heart. She was his dream. His *not impossible she*.

And now she was standing there in the garden, blooming with her husband's baby. And finally, totally, out of his reach.

What had Al said? 'Marriages end. Don't give up hope.' Was that it?

But looking at Abby, so happily in love, so fulfilled, Niall must know there was no hope for him.

He must be so *hurt*, thought Jemima. Her heart turned over as if his pain were her own.

Bloody Pepper, bloody wedding guests, bloody Abigail. Between them, they have cut my love to the heart.

She was across the garden to save him before she had time to think how this was going to hurt her too.

Somehow it didn't matter. Somehow all that mattered was that he should have someone beside him. If he was going to have to say goodbye to The One Woman, he wouldn't have to do it in front of a crowd of curious strangers. He would do it with a friend to hold his hand. A friend who knew the pain of love as well as he did himself.

And that was when she acknowledged it at last. Reluctantly. A little ruefully. With resignation. Walking across a summer-scented garden with rose pollen on her fingers and her heart in her eyes.

I'm a one-man woman. Damn it. And Niall Blackthorne is it.

It was a terrifying thought. She could just see the head-lines: *The Duke and the Tramp.* Well, maybe not a tramp exactly. But—what was it that Niall had called her? A sub-stitute for a coat hanger? It wasn't exactly aristocratic.

But what did aristocracy matter? Niall, she remembered, had kept on sending her messages, though she had never responded. Hell, he had even sent her a mango. She had cried over that, remembering their magical day.

Why would she cry if she didn't love him?

And then the thought came—why would he send it if he didn't love me? A little, anyway. Maybe I'm not the woman of his dreams. But he did love me a little that day on the boat. He did say, *For a day you were mine.* Surely that counts for something.

She was three steps away from him, looking at the back of his head. Jemima swallowed. She was about to risk the biggest brush-off of her life. And she minded; she really did. But she didn't have any choice and she knew it.

She took a deep breath, squared her shoulders, and stepped up to his side.

'Niall,' she said, slipping her hand into his, as she had done on the beach all those months ago. 'I didn't know you were coming.'

He looked down at her, startled.

He was thinner, she thought. Or maybe it was the grey tailcoat. Something made him seem taller and thinner and more formidable, somehow. Unreadable, certainly. She ached for her sexy beach bum with his disgraceful shorts and his laughter. Even for the devil-may-care guy in jeans who had turned up at the flat, before she hacked him to pieces with her nasty tongue. If he was a cool-eyed stranger now, it was her own fault. For a moment Jemima quailed.

She did not let it show. 'Great to see you,' she said, projecting enough warmth to light a barbecue.

Niall's eyebrows twitched together. 'Jemima,' he said cautiously.

She beamed love and support at him. 'Call me Jay Jay. How have you been?'

He did not look at Abby. Oh, how he must hurt. Sure, he felt something for Jemima. But Abby was still his *not impossible she*.

I am going to show him there's an alternative. That people can fall in love a second time, Jemima vowed. He won't come round at first. But in time he will see that what he feels for me is enough.

But, still, she could have wept for what he must be feeling now.

'Fine, thank you,' said Niall, still wary.

Abby said, 'Oh, it's so exciting. He's a hero, Jay Jay. He's been busting criminals.'

It was the last thing she had expected. 'What?'

Niall looked uncomfortable. 'Not all on my own, Ab.'

The pet name stabbed Jemima as viciously as a sudden blow from a stiletto. Neither of them even noticed it, she thought. Intimacy just came so naturally to them.

Oh, this was hopeless. Abby was just so utterly entwined in his heart and mind there was nothing anyone else could do to help.

She withdrew her hand from his. Or she tried to. Only his fingers tightened like a vice and she couldn't move. She turned her head, shocked, and found that he wasn't unreadable any more. His eyes gleamed. The sexy beach bum was clearly still alive and kicking under the elegant morning clothes.

Her exquisitely made-up cheeks warmed.

For a day you were mine. Maybe—more than a day?

'He's been tracking money launderers,' burbled Abby, oblivious.

Jemima tried hard to be interested. He had started to rotate his thumb in that secret place in the centre of her palm, and it was nigh on impossible to concentrate on anything else. But she did her best.

'I thought you were a gambler,' she said breathlessly.

'I am. I was only moonlighting as a cop.'

'I don't understand.'

Niall shrugged indifferently. But the wicked thumb still did its work, telling her that he was not indifferent at all.

Jemima's insides began to turn to treacle. Warm treacle.

'Money launderers often use casinos to pass funds around. You can't trace the stuff back anywhere because nobody has paid it to you for anything. It just looks as if you won it. Rather clever. So I watched who won more than the average. And who lost. And then tried to see if they were working together.'

'It must have been so exciting,' said Abby, thrilled. 'Were you in danger?'

'Only from passing redheads.'

Jemima choked.

Abby was delighted. 'A honey trap. Isn't that what they call it? Were they on to you, then?'

'No. But there was a point when I thought they were.'

He looked at Jemima very steadily. 'This woman turned up with the thinnest story you'd ever heard.'

'Oh, really?' said Jemima. The thumb was driving her demented and she felt some fighting back was due. 'What did you do about it?'

'Checked her out,' said Niall blandly.

'That must have been hard.'

'It was worth it.'

Has his mouth always been so sensual? She couldn't take her eyes off it. Soon, even cheery Abby was going to notice something.

'And was she all she seemed?' said Jemima breathlessly.

'Oh, a lot more. A whole lot more.'

The dark eyes took on a brooding look. Suddenly she remembered the feel of his mouth against her heated skin; the brilliant sky above; the smell of the boat; the swish of the waves. And the totally absorbed lover worshipping her body as if they had belonged together since the beginning of time.

For a day you were mine. Could a day turn into for ever?

Jemima was having difficulty in breathing. She cleared her throat.

'Was that a good thing?'

'I thought so at the time.'

Abby said, 'Don't tell me you've been seducing a master spy, Niall?'

Jemima could have groaned aloud. Oh, God, how could the woman be so blind?

Niall laughed suddenly and stopped teasing. 'You're just too easy to wind up, Ab. I took notes and made a few phone calls. It really wasn't glamorous at all.'

'Oh, you,' she said indulgently. 'I'd better go and find my husband. The junior bridesmaid showed signs of kidnapping him to go and play tennis.'

'Then rescue him at once,' advised Jemima. 'The junior bridesmaid is a force to be reckoned with.'

Abby lifted a hand in farewell and went.

Left alone with her, Niall tugged her round to face him.

'You look amazing,' he said huskily.

Jemima had driven fashion writers to rave reviews and poetry for five years. But she blushed.

'Wedding finery,' she said. 'Of course clean hair helps.'

He chuckled, and touched the masses of dark red silk. His fingers were not reverent. But they were gentle, respectful. His touch said, I have the right to stroke your hair. You have given me that right.

Jemima's lips parted

'You take my breath away,' he told her.

She hardly dared to believe him. But there was a caressing look in the ugly-handsome face which even she, with all her doubts, could not mistake.

'I must talk to you,' he said. 'Where can we go?'

She cast about for a solution. 'Well, there's a sort of private garden. We were taking photographs by the roses. But it's full of happy snappers.'

Niall's chin jutted. 'Not for long.'

He marched her into the walled garden and rounded up the amateur photographers with the kind but firm determination of an expert sheepdog.

'Food's being served. Better go before it's all gone,' he said.

They believed him. They went.

He shut the ironwork gate behind them and turned the big key in the lock.

'I hope you haven't locked us in for ever. That key looks awfully old,' Jemima pointed out.

'I don't care. I'll build you a shelter and we can live off rosehips and rainwater,' said Niall, alluringly driven to poetry. 'Oh, my darling, my darling, my darling, I thought I'd lost you for ever.'

And he hauled her into his arms like a drowning man.

His kisses were just as she remembered. No—more than she remembered. There hadn't been that wild intensity before. It made him a little clumsy. And a hundred times more passionate.

'I'm a fool,' said Niall. 'A crass, unkind, fool. Telling you all about my adolescent first love when I should have been saying, You're the light of life, stay with me.'

Jemima was trembling. 'What?'

'My only excuse,' he said, 'is I'm not good with feelings. Give me a card table—or a boat—or anything practical—and I can do anything with it. But tell the woman of my dreams I need her? Forget it.'

'Woman of your dreams?' faltered Jemima. 'But that's Abby. You and she—you're the same sort of people. She's like you. She wants a big house and horses and stuff.'

Niall stared at her unflatteringly. 'That is such twaddle,' he said, a lot less poetic all of a sudden.

'She's even got a title,' said Jemima, distracted. 'Whereas I'm your instant celebrity, just trading on my looks. No substance to me at all.'

Niall let her go. 'The only thing that's wrong with you is you're a snob.'

That brought her out of her distraction. 'What? I'm not. How dare you?'

'Yes, you are. You were in love with me when you didn't know I was a duke,' he said smugly.

Jemima prudently decided to ignore the first part of that. 'Come to that, why didn't you tell me you were a duke?

His face clouded. 'I would have got round to it. Only I was still getting used to the idea myself. And I had the money laundering job to finish before I came back and took up the reins.'

'You didn't want to come back to England,' said Jemima sadly. 'Because that was where Abby lived. And you couldn't have Abby.'

Niall groaned. 'Oh, boy, you really have bought my retarded emotions hook, line and sinker, haven't you?'

She shook her head, not understanding.

'Well, I have only myself to blame,' muttered Niall. 'Listen to me, you beautiful revelation, you saved me from wandering around like something out of bad Victorian poetry, telling myself my heart was broken for the rest of my life. You made me want you. Then you made me love you. Then you made me do months of hard labour when you walked out on me. Enough, already. Will you please stop messing with my head and do the decent thing? You know you want it too.'

He was laughing, but the look in his eyes was very, very serious. Jemima's hands went out to him in pure instinct.

But he had called her a snob. And he hadn't told her he was a duke. There was a need for some redress in the power balance here.

She hung back, her brown eyes glinting gold in the sun.

'Let me get this straight. Are you asking me to marry you?'

He raised his eyes to heaven. 'Trying to, God help me. Trying to.'

It was a gift. Jemima's eyes danced.

'Try harder,' she said.

So he did.

EPILOGUE

'MADAME was furious,' Jemima told Niall.

They were walking along the untidy harbour at sunset. The air hummed with warmth.

Her hair was loose and fragrant in the breeze. Niall turned to nuzzle it luxuriously.

'Mmm.'

She chuckled. 'She was so pleased with me for netting a duke. She'd already put out the wedding dress to tender. Even when I told her we were getting married in the Caribbean, she still thought she could mastermind the party.'

'I could have told her she wouldn't,' Niall said calmly. 'When you set your heart on something you're unstoppable.'

'Just as well I set my heart on you, then.'

'I give thanks for it every day.' But although his voice was light she knew it was a truth too deep to dwell on.

She hugged his arm. 'Me too.'

He looked down at her, his face almost unrecognisable with the love blazing out of him.

'And you're sure you don't mind? Giving up all the stuff of a big wedding?'

'I,' said Jemima with feeling, 'have had enough big weddings to last me a lifetime. I want to share something you did.'

They had got to the side of the vessel they were travelling on. It was stained and shabby and to her it looked like heaven.

'After all, I don't know anyone who has got married on a banana boat,' she said wickedly. 'I'll be able to loll around in bed all day, while you show off your muscles hauling crates of bananas.'

'Any lolling, we do together,' said Niall firmly.

He kissed her hard.

'Yes, please.' There was that sexy little catch in her voice which always made his collar feel too tight.

'Siren,' he said fondly. 'Oh, by the way, I've got something to give to you.'

She was intrigued. 'Some ducal heirloom?' she teased.

'No. An heirloom of our own,' he said mysteriously. 'Something to remind me that I nearly missed the real thing because I'd got too used to the old fairy story.'

It had taken him a long time to convince Jemima that she wasn't a second-best substitute for his imaginary Abby, but he had done it at last.

She punched him playfully. 'Oh, you! What is it? Don't keep me in suspense.'

And from out of his pocket he produced two scraps of material in day-glo turquoise and cerise.

'My bikini,' cried Jemima, choking with delight. 'Oh, I'm so glad you found another one. I was so stupid, throwing it away like that. Only I was so hurt...'

He stopped her and took her face between his hands.

'I know you were, my love. And it was my fault.'

'Not entirely.'

'Mostly.' He held her strongly. 'I can't promise that I won't ever hurt you again. But if I'm being stupid and blind come and put that damned bikini in front of me. And I'll do better.'

'Oh, my love,' said Jemima, moved.

The long, slow, passionate kiss was much admired by the crew of the banana boat, connoisseurs of kisses to a man.

And later, after they had put out to sea and the captain had married them under the stars, holding high an old-fashioned hurricane lamp so he could read the service, Niall took her down to the small passenger cabin and made love to her with his whole heart.

Only at the end, as she lay in delicious exhaustion in his arms, did he say smugly, 'Oh, by the way. It wasn't another one.'

'What?' said Jemima, caressing him, drowsy and shameless.

'The bikini. I went into your room and liberated it. It's the real thing.'

She lifted herself up and stared at him, amazed. *'What?'*

'The real thing. Like us,' he said soberly, holding her against his heart. 'Just like us.'

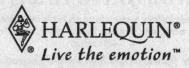